T0208937

The Artificial Evolution

They look like us. Act like us. But they are not human. Created to perform the menial tasks real humans detest, Synths were designed with only a basic intelligence and minimal emotional response. It stands to reason that they have no rights. Like any technology, they are designed for human convenience. Disposable.

In the city of New Lyons, Detective Jason Campbell is investigating a vicious crime: a female body found mutilated and left in the streets. Once the victim is identified as a Synth, the crime is designated no more than the destruction of property, and Campbell is pulled from the case.

But when a mysterious stranger approaches Campbell and asks him to continue his investigation in secret, Campbell is dragged into a dark world of unimaginable corruption. One that leaves him questioning the true nature of humanity.

And what he discovers is only the beginning . . .

SINthetic

J. T. Nicholas

REBEL BASE BOOKS
Kensington Publishing Corp.
www.kensingtonbooks.com

Rebel Base Books are published by
Kensington Publishing Corp. 119 West 40th Street New York, NY 10018

All Kensington titles, imprints, and distributed lines are available at special quantity discounts for bulk purchases for sales promotion, premiums, fund-raising, and educational or institutional use.

Special book excerpts or customized printings can also be created to fit specific needs. For details, write or phone the office of the Kensington Special Sales Manager:
Kensington Publishing Corp.
119 West 40th Street
New York, NY 10018
Attn. Special Sales Department. Phone: 1-800-221-2647.

Kensington Reg. U.S. Pat. & TM Off.
REBEL BASE Reg. U.S. Pat. & TM Off.
The RB logo is a trademark of Kensington Publishing Corp.

First Electronic Edition: January 2018
eISBN-13: 978-1-63573-004-3
eISBN-10: 1-63573-004-X

First Print Edition: January 2018
ISBN-13: 978-1-63573-007-4
ISBN-10: 1-63573-007-4

Printed in the United States of America

For Julie, who encouraged me to keep going no matter how many rejections poured in. You're twenty books ahead, but I'm catching up fast.

When bad men combine, the good must associate; else they will fall, one by one, an unpitied sacrifice in a contemptible struggle.

~ Edmund Burke, circa 1770

Bad men need nothing more to compass their ends, than that good men should look on and do nothing.

~ John Stuart Mill, circa 1867

Chapter 1

The neon signs glowed sullenly, sending sickly tendrils of light slithering down the rain-soaked streets like so many diseased serpents. Once bright and inviting, the reds and blues and greens had dimmed and paled, sloughed off the flush of health, and left behind a spreading stain of false illumination that heralded nothing but sickness and decay. The signs themselves, flickering and buzzing, wheezing like something that wanted to die, something that *should* have died long ago, offered up a thousand different sins, unflinching in the frank descriptions of the acts taking place within the walls that they adorned.

I stared at those signs, indistinct and hazy beneath the mantle of falling rain. The mist softened their lurid offers, restoring, however imperfectly, an innocence the city lost long ago. As the gentle caress of a silken veil added mystery to the sweeping curves of the female form, hinting at secrets far more tantalizing than the revealed flesh beneath, the cloak of rainfall shrouded the city's darker side, softening its edges and lending it an air that approached civility.

Approached civility, but did not—could not—achieve it.

With a sigh, I turned my eyes away from the cityscape, and dropped them to the pavement beneath my feet. To the body that rested there, or what was left of it.

After nearly ten years on the job, I still had to fight down the bile threatening to crawl its way up my esophagus and force its insistent path between my teeth. The body—so much easier to think of it as "the body" and not "the woman"—lay flat on its back, arms stretched out above its head and crossed at the wrists, legs spread akimbo. No clothing. Nor could I see any discarded garments in the immediate area. The pose, purposeful and meticulous in its own horrifying way, was a parody of passion. It was a pose that was likely even now being played out in many, perhaps most, of the establishments adorned with the gasping neon signs.

With one very notable difference.

Vestiges of beauty clung to the woman, holding desperately to a youthful vivacity that was losing an inexorable battle to the unnatural slackness of death. Makeup adorned that face, hiding the pallor beneath blush and eyeliner, lipstick and shadow, only now beginning to fade and run beneath the unrelenting assault of a thousand raindrops. Her features were symmetrical, regular, past the awkwardness of youth, but not yet touched by the wrinkles or worry lines that would fell all of us in time.

I forced myself to look past her face, past the strong lines of her outstretched arms, sweeping past her bared breasts and to the…emptiness… that extended beneath her sternum.

From her lowest ribs to the tops of her thighs, the woman had been…

I realized I didn't have a word for what had been done to her. The words that stormed through my mind—savaged, brutalized, tortured—leaving a teeth-gnashing anger in their wake and making my stomach twist itself into a Stygian knot, were almost certainly true, but they did not describe what lay before me.

Hollowed.

The word floated up from somewhere in my subconscious, bringing with it memories of carving into pumpkins and scooping out the seeds and ropey innards with big plastic spoons made slick and awkward from the pulpy mess.

I clamped my teeth so hard that a lance of pain shot along my sinus cavities, but it kept me—if only just—from vomiting.

Hollowed.

The skin and muscle had been removed from the woman's stomach and groin. The organs that should have been present—stomach, intestines, kidneys, everything south of the lungs—were gone. The tissue beneath them, the muscles along the spine, back, and buttocks remained, exposed to the air and rain. I could just make out pinkish gray tissue poking from beneath the ribs, so I guessed the lungs, and probably the heart, were intact and in place.

There was no blood.

The steady rain had formed a small pool in the resulting cavity, taking on a cast more black than red in the dimness of the night. No more blood on the body. No more blood at the scene.

"Holy Mary, Mother of God."

The heartfelt exhalation came from behind me, and I glanced over my shoulder, tearing my eyes from the horror before me. The uniforms had finished cordoning off the area, spreading the yellow tape in a rough perimeter maybe twenty yards in diameter. Even on a night like this, in a neighborhood like this, a crowd had gathered, a few dozen people pressed up against the tape as if it were the glass wall at an aquarium, desperate to peer into the darkness and see the wonders and horrors within. All of them pointed screens in my direction or stared with the strange motionless intensity of someone wearing a recording lens. I prayed that the darkness, rain, and distance would cloud their electronic eyes, and grant the woman what little privacy and modesty were left to her.

Halfway between me and the tape stood a small, trim man in his late forties. A fuzz of iron-gray hair sprouted from his head like a fungus, and a pencil-thin beard traced the line of his jaw. He wore blue coveralls, stenciled with the words "Medical Examiner" in gold thread. Dr. Clarence Fitzpatrick had been medical examiner in New Lyons for longer than I'd been a cop. We had worked some gruesome homicides, scenes far messier, at least in terms of scattered gore, than what lay before us. But nothing quite so damn eerie.

"Yeah," I muttered. "What can you tell me?"

He made his way to the body and knelt by it, blue-gloved hands extended over it as if trying to divine information from the ether. "Liver temp is out of the question," he said. There was no humor in his voice, no attempt to make light of the nature of the remains; he was simply stating the facts of the case before him, retreating behind cold professionalism. It was something you learned quick on the job. Those who could not put a wall between the atrocities and their own souls never lasted long.

He touched the flesh of the woman's arm, pressing against it, feeling the elasticity. "No rigor mortis, which means that death was either very recent or she's been gone awhile."

He panned a flashlight across the body, the pale flesh luminescing under the harsh white light. "No discoloration of the remaining tissue. The damage sustained to the torso is sufficient to cause death, but there is no way to tell in situ if that occurred before or after she expired. Though if it had been done here, we would certainly be seeing a lot more blood, even with the rain." He spoke in short, clipped bursts, keeping the medical jargon to a minimum, for my benefit no doubt.

His hands moved to the woman's head, peeling back the eyelids. "Cloudy. Most likely, she was killed more than twelve, but less than forty-eight hours ago. Apart from the obvious evisceration, there is no readily identifiable cause of death." He cupped the woman's face in his hands, twisting it gently to the side, continuing his field examination. He brushed back the dark locks of her hair, revealing the back of her neck. A deep sigh, a sound of relief, not regret, escaped him. "Thank God," he said.

I stared down at the woman, not really seeing what the doctor saw, but I knew what would be there. Only one thing could have drawn that reaction from Fitzpatrick. A raised pattern of flesh, roughly the size of an old postage stamp, darker than the surrounding skin and looking for all the world like an antiquated bar code. The tissue would be reminiscent of ritualistic scarring, but, unlike the woman herself, would not have known the touch of violence. It could be called a birthmark, but "birth" was not a word applied to the lab-grown people that were, collectively, known as synthetics. They bore other names, of course, dozens of them, all derogatory, all aimed at dehumanizing them further, at driving home the point that, though they might look and act and feel like us, they were *not* humans.

Dr. Fitzpatrick was not immune to that dehumanization. "Thank God," he said again. "She's a mule."

Chapter 2

"You hear me, Campbell?"

Fitzpatrick was staring at me, the dead woman's—the synthetic's—head still clutched in his hands. His grip, I noted, had changed, losing any sense of tenderness, any hint of care. He might as well have been holding a basketball or a cantaloupe.

"Yeah, I heard you."

"Good." He stood up, pulling the gloves off one at a time with an audible snap. "Then I guess I'm done here."

"Fitzpatrick, wait," I said, out of pure reflex. He looked at me, one eyebrow raised in silent surprise.

Under the law, synthetics didn't have rights. They were less than people on a level so profound that they were relegated to objects, to things. If you found a broken toaster in the middle of the street, you didn't call the police, or the medical examiner. You kicked it to the curb and trusted that the sanitation department would catch it in their next sweep. NLPD wouldn't just leave a body—even a synthetic—for the garbage men, of course. Artificially created or not, the corpse of a synthetic was subject to the same laws of decomposition as every other organism, and there was a public health issue with leaving it rotting in the streets. No, it would be removed by the paramedic crews, taken to the closest morgue, and, by law, cremated as soon as—no pun intended—humanly possible.

Taking with it any and all evidence that might help me find out who had done this to the poor girl.

"I want a postmortem done on the synthetic," I said, trying to keep my voice emotionless.

"What? Sorry, Campbell, but I've got enough real bodies back in cold storage that need my attention. I don't have time to go playing doctor on someone else's toy." The words were cold, callous, and, at the same time, probing.

I clamped my teeth on the angry retort that tried to burst forth. I had a reputation at the precinct, one that had stuck with me since my military days. It didn't matter that my juvenile record had been not just sealed, but expunged, or that nothing in my actual service record showed anything out of the ordinary...well, at least if you didn't count the large number of "redacted for national security" items as extraordinary. Somewhere along the line, I'd been labeled a synth-sympathizer, one of those people who held the delusional—at least according to society—belief that synthetics were real people and deserved to be treated as such. Most of the time, the rumors earned me nothing more than the occasional sideways glance, but anytime something came up involving a synthetic, those glances got a certain "torches and pitchforks" look about them.

I stared down at the body, and couldn't help but see another girl, another pool of blood. I'd seen so many. So many bodies. My time as a soldier could be measured in the dead. The endless wars over whatever radical ideology was the enemy du jour and the equally endless disaster relief work stemming from the kinds of superstorms that had finally sunk New Orleans. My time as a cop had been better, but still measured in blood. Fuck. I couldn't just let it go.

"Look, Fitzpatrick, I know she's a mule." I hated the term—a derogatory reference to the sterility inherent in the synthetics—but I used it anyway. "But this isn't normal. If someone wants to carve up their toys in the privacy of their own home, and then dispose of the...remains...appropriately, that's fine." It wasn't fine. It was a long damn way from fine and it made me feel like eight layers of sleaze to say it, but I kept on. "But whoever did this left a big damn mess for someone else to clean up. You don't do that unless you want attention. And anyone who wants attention that bad won't be content to play with toys for very long." I shrugged, trying to make the gesture as casual as possible. "Honestly, I'd be far more concerned if I thought the perp was a synth, but if someone's working their way up to the majors, we need to know."

"Impossible," Fitzpatrick announced at once. "The programming of the synthetics is clear. They can't harm us. Their purpose is to serve and obey. It's fascinating, actually. I wish I understood the process better, but Walton Biogenics doesn't release much information on their products." He came to an abrupt stop as he caught the look on my face, no doubt realizing he had started to ramble. Fitzpatrick was clearly interested in the topic, and why wouldn't he be? Synthetic tissue had been a part of the medical field for decades, but when it came to full-fledged synthetic life Walton Biogenics made sure that they kept the secrets of synthetics locked down tight, so competitors and potential black marketers couldn't edge in on their profit margins.

"Still..." Fitzpatrick's eyes had narrowed, and a frown tugged the corners of his lips. He wasn't convinced, but he hadn't walked away, either, and I could tell that the thought of a synthetic in his lab intrigued him. He wasn't a bad guy, really. Just another government slug, doing his job as best he could. The only thing he seemed to take any joy in was shepherding along his assistants; less, I thought, from seeing them do well, and more from the sense of pride he took in being the one who helped them get there. Which gave me another tack to take.

"Look, Doctor," I said, making the honorific as respectful as I could, "I want to find out who did this and make sure they don't need to be put in a nice, safe, rubber room before they start cutting *real* people. You don't have to do the autopsy yourself. No laws or regulations getting in the way of one of your assistants working unsupervised on a synthetic, right? You can even look at it as a test for one of them—an odd case, lots of missing parts, very little in the way of physical evidence. What can they find out on their own?" I gave him a conspiratorial grin.

Fitzpatrick arched a single eyebrow. "Why do I get the feeling, Detective, that you are playing me?" I met his look, keeping the grin on my face and giving him the smallest suggestion of a shrug. The medical examiner was a smart man, but even the smartest of men could get caught up in their own ego.

"Still," he said at last, "it *is* a very interesting idea, and certainly a most unusual case. You understand that my assistants are not medical doctors, and none of them are fully trained. They may well miss some vital piece of evidence."

I wasn't exactly spoiled for choice. "I understand, Doctor. But they've been trained by the best. I've got complete faith in whoever you assign." I worried, for a moment, that I had laid it on too thick, but, apparently, that wasn't possible. A genuine smile split Fitzpatrick's face and I could almost see the gears turning in his head as he cycled through his assistants, trying to pick out the one best suited for the task.

"Very well, then. It will be an interesting experiment, to be sure."

Fitzpatrick gave me a curt nod, and then bustled off, grabbing a pair of paramedics and giving them detailed instructions on dealing with the remains. I felt a slight thrill of relief course through me. It wasn't a huge victory, but sometimes the little win was all you could count on.

There wasn't much left to do at the scene. The synthetic's ID could be pulled easily enough—that's what the tags were for, after all. It would be the first thing Fitzpatrick's assistant—whichever one won the prize of performing the autopsy—would do, so I'd have that information soon enough. The uniforms were checking the area, and a few were conducting knock-and-talks along the rows of liquor stores, synth-brothels, and worse, but I knew that no one would have seen anything. In this type of neighborhood, no one ever did.

I turned the scene over to the uniforms and climbed into my car. I reclined the seat as far as it would go, lying nearly flat. "Home," I said, throwing one arm over my eyes.

"Voice recognition confirmed," the car replied in a toneless, androgynous voice. "Destination: home. Is this correct?"

"Yeah," I growled.

The engine—electric—started with a faint hum, joined in a moment by the *thrum-thrum-thrum* of the windshield wipers. Why the self-driving vehicle even bothered with wipers was beyond me. Unless I took manual control, there was no need for windows at all, but sometimes necessities from the past clung desperately to the present.

As the car accelerated, I pulled out my screen and tapped my news app. The video started at once, and with a flick, I sent it to the interior of the windshield. The transparent glass immediately changed, going momentarily black and then filling with the image of a newsroom. The anchors, one male, one female, sat behind a curved desk. Both were attractive, but lacking in the perfect bilateral symmetry common to synthetics...and made normal humans seem almost bland in comparison. The broadcast wasn't live—only truly monumental events ever were, anymore. Instead, the feed that I was watching was an amalgam of previously recorded segments, automatically selected by the filters I had set in place and edited into a seamless video that was almost indistinguishable from a continuous feed.

"SynthFirst," the female newscaster was saying, her broad smile dripping with condescension, "the fringe group that insists synthetics are human, attempted to file yet another lawsuit with the Fifth Circuit Court today, claiming infringement of the constitutional rights of synthetics. The filing was dismissed out of hand, citing lack of grounds due to the legal classification of synthetics. The court also ruled SynthFirst in contempt for their constant, and I quote, 'spurious and frivolous lawsuits wasting the court's time over a matter that had been settled decades ago.' SynthFirst insists that they will continue to bring suits, despite the fines levied against them. Tom?"

The camera shifted to the other anchor. "Thanks, June. In other news..."

Whatever the reason, the constant patter of raindrops on the car, the whir of the road beneath the tires, and the droning of the news broadcast... all of it instilled in me a deep, irresistible lethargy.

I let my eyes drift close, the gentle lullaby of the wipers guiding me down into a fitful sleep.

Chapter 3

A soft chime from the car, indicating that I was nearing my destination, startled me to wakefulness. I rubbed at my eyes with the heels of my palms, trying to scrub the image of a dead girl from the corners of my mind. With the push of a button, I returned the seat to the upright position and peered out the window. The soft rain still fell, streaking the driver's-side window like endless tears. The car was passing over the Madison Bridge, leaving behind the dry land portion of New Lyons and heading into Floattown. The waters of Chandeleur Sound, ever unsettled, ebbed and flowed far beneath the bridge, the surge of the waves causing miniature whirlpools to form around the massive concrete pilings.

I watched as bridge and waters alike slid beneath the car, letting the hiss of wet pavement fill my mind. Anything to keep it from returning to the image of the murdered, eviscerated synthetic. Anything to keep it from reaching even deeper into memory to pull forth the image of another dead girl.

The car bounced gently as it transitioned from the bridge to Floattown proper. Or rather, to the bridgehead from which the rest of Floattown blossomed. Technically, the bridgehead was Ile Beton, the Concrete Island, a massive feat of engineering that had created a slug of steel and concrete several hundred yards across and dozens of feet above sea level and sunk it into the ocean floor. But that man-made island held only a small percentage of the population of Floattown. Dozens of broad, gentle stairways led from the edge of the bridgehead and down to the actual district.

The car parked itself in my reserved space—one of the few perks of being a detective. I climbed wearily from the vehicle and walked to the nearest stairway. I stood for a moment, admiring the view. It wasn't pretty. There's not a lot that can make a hundred or so pontoon-supported platforms—cleverly dubbed VLFSs for "very large floating structures"—sprouting cheap prefabricated buildings, pretty. But the fact that an area of ocean the size of several city blocks had been reclaimed and now supported thousands was a testament to the human spirit. Sure, rising waters and storm surge might have put paid to the city that had stood here decades ago, but Mother Nature herself couldn't stop mankind from rebuilding. Floattown rested over the bones of what had been New Orleans, and every day more VLFSs came that much closer to completion. Something about that refusal to surrender no matter the odds gave me just a little bit of hope that, despite everything, our species wasn't doomed.

Which was why, despite being able to afford better, I chose to live in a neighborhood that was considered one of the worst in the city. Besides, it kept certain skills honed to a nice edge; that edge could still mean the difference between life and death. I had no intention of letting it grow dull.

I shook my head to clear the sleep from it, and felt the familiar tingle along my spine as I set foot on the first of the wide stairs. My right hand hung loose and ready, close to the service pistol riding in a paddle holster at my hip. The streets of Floattown were safe enough during the day—kids played in the streets and people went about their daily lives—but it was almost two in the morning, and after midnight, the seedier elements came out.

I moved briskly down the stairs and onto the first of the floating platforms, eyes sweeping left and right. Floattown was built to be self-contained, with the residential areas nestled above and between shops, convenience stores, bodegas, and restaurants. It had the potential to be as great as any thriving urban neighborhood...but the aesthetically boring and repetitive architecture of the prefab structures and the subtle but omnipresent shifting of the platforms had kept all but the impoverished away. Most were good people, some working hard to get ahead, others content scratching by on just the government-issued stipend—but in both cases, honest people trying to live their lives. A few, though, dabbled in crime, some petty street crime like vandalism, with others organizing into gangs that dealt in what few black and gray market items remained. Guns, for the most part, and stolen property, and the very few drugs that were cheaper and easier to get from the local dealer than the local corner store.

The streets were largely empty, but here and there small groups gathered, at a street corner or within the shrouded gloom of a building's front stoop. I made sure to meet the eyes of each person I passed. Part of that was to get a read on the potential danger—you could tell a lot about a person from their eyes—but it was also a declaration, "I'm not prey."

The hair on the back of my neck stirred, and I turned, hand automatically seeking the butt of my pistol. My eyes scanned the street around me, but there was nothing. Just apartment buildings, most with at least a single light burning on their front stoops, and the steady, rhythmic lap of the waves. I didn't turn back around, not immediately. Instead, I stood there, waiting. In the distance, a dog started barking. I eased my hand away from my gun, and turned around again, once more putting one foot in front of the other.

The feeling, like someone running their fingers along the nape of my neck, stuck with me as I made my way to my apartment building. I kept my eyes open, seeking, scanning, paying close attention to any reflective surface, hoping to catch a glimpse of whatever had my guard up.

I saw nothing.

By the time I reached the low, squat apartment building that I called home, my heart was thudding in my chest and my fingers kept twitching toward my sidearm. Sure, Floattown wasn't the best neighborhood, but it was *my* neighborhood. I'd walked the streets later than this and never felt the kind of near panic that was clawing at me now. I was armed, and trained by both the military and the police. The local thugs were tough, but none of them had seen any action more significant than a drive-by.

I pressed my palm against the security pad at the main door to the apartment building. There was a momentary hesitation, followed by a faint beep and the click of the magnetic lock disengaging. I pulled the door open and slipped inside, waiting to ensure the door latched firmly behind me. It wasn't a huge structure—nothing was on the floating platforms. Just a squat, squarish three-story building with four apartments per floor. The hallway lights burned bright and steady as I made my way up the stairs. Mine was apartment six, second on the right on the second floor. I palmed the lock here as well. The sound of bolts disengaging was no mere click, but a heavy, meaty *thunk*.

I pushed the door open and stepped into my living room. Long habit had me tossing my wallet and badge onto the table next to the door and saying, "Lights," before anything else really registered. As the overheads flicked on, I spotted the pale, hulking form sitting in my armchair.

Reflex took over, and I had my pistol out and trained on the man before I even really saw him. "Right there!" I barked, slipping into my cop voice. "Don't move. Keep your hands where I can see them."

"That is hardly necessary."

The words were a low, deep baritone, hovering right on the edge of bass. The man hadn't moved, hadn't reacted at all to the barrel of the forty-five pointed at his chest. He sat there, hands on the armrests of the chair, face composed, as if this was his home and I was the entertainment.

The adrenaline was still pumping, but the sense of immediate danger waned. I had the guy dead to rights, and we both knew it. There was no way he could get out of that seat and reach me—or draw a weapon for that matter—before I could Mozambique him. That gave me my first chance to really look at him.

He had skin so pale it was almost white—like a fresh sheet of paper. He kept his eyes narrowed against even the faint light of my apartment, but I saw that the irises were a pale, pinkish red. He was clean shaven—no, not clean shaven. Hairless. No hair on his head, no eyebrows, no stubble, and no sign that there ever *had* been any hair there. I couldn't be certain in the poor light and with his coloration, but it didn't even look like he had eyelashes. He did, however, have massive shoulders, wide and rounded like boulders, filling a chair that could have comfortably held two of me. They framed a barrel chest, and sprouted heavily muscled arms ending in broad, blunt hands. He was dressed casually, a simple black T-shirt that stretched tight over his frame and faded blue jeans, with a pair of heavy leather work boots on his feet. A khaki raincoat and matching fedora were folded neatly on the table before him.

He wasn't human.

"How did you get in here?" I demanded, keeping the gun leveled. He might be calm, but he was also big. Synthetics weren't supposed to be able to hurt us, but then, they weren't supposed to be able to commit petty crimes, like breaking and entering, or trespassing, either. I wasn't in the mood to take chances.

Those massive shoulders lifted, fell. "I have a way with electronics. You wouldn't know it to look at me, of course." He smiled self-deprecatingly, revealing uneven, yellowed teeth. Strange, for a synthetic. They always seemed to have perfect teeth. "I'm not here to hurt you," he added, acknowledging the gun at last.

"You shouldn't be *able* to hurt me," I growled, keeping my weapon trained on center mass. "Any more than you should be able to be here in the first place."

"Ah, yes. The vaunted programming of the synthetics. Well," he continued, "like any conditioning, it can be broken, given enough time, effort, and desire."

"Fascinating. Really. But what the hell are you doing here?" I demanded. The adrenaline was wearing off, and I felt a slight tremor in my hands. The fully loaded forty-five weighed a little over three pounds. Not very much, until you had to hold it at arm's length for a while. Shit. I drew a deep breath and steadied my hands by force of will, keeping the gun leveled.

He tilted his head to one side. "Do you know what I am?"

"Yeah," I said. "You're a synthetic."

"But do you know what kind?"

It was a strange question, but an easy enough one. The short stature, broad shoulders, albinism, all of them pointed to a synthetic designed to spend a lot of time underground, in areas with low overhead. In other parts of the country, he might be a miner, but not here. "You're a tunnel worker," I guessed. "Sanitation, probably. Which doesn't explain what the fuck you're doing in my house."

He smiled again. "You are a strange one, Detective Campbell. You are correct in your assessment, but you answer in a way different from almost every human I have ever encountered." He paused, as if in thought. Then he cocked his head and said, "Tell me, Detective, if one of your friends with the NLPD walked into their house and found that I, a synthetic, had broken into their home, what would they do?"

The answer came unbidden to my lips, and I said the single word before I really thought about it. "Shoot."

"Yes," the synthetic agreed. "Without question. Without hesitation. And yet, here we are, having an almost civilized conversation. You haven't even ordered me from your home. Why is that, Detective?"

I said nothing, and for a long moment, the synthetic seemed content with the silence.

"Sewer rat," he said at last.

The non sequitur threw me, and the gun wavered again. "What?"

"Sewer rat. That is what most of your kind would call me. Mules, toys... how many names do you have for us?"

Dozens, but there was fuck all I could do about it. I was tired, angry, and had a persistent twisting in my stomach that felt too much like guilt to ignore. It pissed me off. "What do you want?" I demanded.

"To help you."

The words surprised me enough that I almost lowered the gun. Almost. "What the hell are you talking about?"

"You are different, Detective. I've been looking for someone like you for a long time. A very long time." A faint shudder coursed through me at the way he said the words. There was something almost...religious about his tone. I eyed him again and realized that I had no real way of knowing his age. All of the normal markers were masked by his odd physical characteristics.

"Great. Help me with what?"

"The girl you found tonight, she wasn't the first."

Another jolt of adrenaline surged through my system at the words; the pistol steadied in my hands and I raised it a bit, bringing the sights back in line with the top of the synthetic's sternum. "What do you know about that? *How* do you know about that?" There wouldn't have been a news report, not for a dead synthetic.

"Those are not the right questions, Detective. The questions you should be asking are 'Why was she mutilated?' and 'Why leave her there in the street?'" He moved one hand slowly, carefully toward his jeans pocket. I took up the slack on the trigger, pulling it almost to the breaking point. But the strange synthetic didn't pull out a weapon. Instead, he removed a piece of paper, folded several times. He placed it on my coffee table, next to his coat and hat. Then he stood, picking up his outerwear, moving with that same careful, casual grace.

"That piece of paper has the names of seven other victims, Detective." A frown of distaste twisted his features. "And their serial numbers. Now, I will take my leave of you."

He didn't move toward me, just looked at me, or maybe past me, at the door. He was relaxed, patient, waiting for me to move or pull the trigger. Seven more victims? Shit. I should detain him, or arrest him, but I couldn't. I couldn't bring a synthetic into the station, couldn't convince anyone that he was a material witness. I couldn't risk calling any attention to the fact that I was working the case at all. And no matter what the big pale fucker said about overcoming conditioning, I seriously doubted he could have killed seven people. Or synthetics. Or whatever.

He was still waiting, eyeing me with those strange red eyes. I edged away from the door, moving along the couch, keeping the pistol trained on him.

He smiled at me again, and strode to the door, pulling it open. As he stepped through, he looked over his shoulder and said, "Remember the questions, Detective. I'll be in touch." The door slipped shut behind him.

I dropped to the couch, putting the pistol on the coffee table next to the folded piece of paper. For a long moment, I just sat there, waiting for the shakes. The adrenaline crash, the spinning, whirling chaos of my mind. It started in my hands, a little tremble that crept up my arms and then spread, until my whole body was shaking uncontrollably, like wave after wave of shivers. It lasted maybe a minute, maybe two. When it passed, I walked over to my kitchen and grabbed a tumbler from the cabinet with still-trembling hands. Three fingers of whiskey splashed into the glass, and I swallowed it in a single gulp. It burned all the way down, but it helped calm my nerves. I poured another three fingers, this time dropping a couple of cubes of ice into the glass for good measure.

I sat in the armchair the synthetic had vacated, and grabbed the piece of paper. I unfolded it, and stared at the seven lines. Seven names, all female. Next to them an alphanumeric series of seemingly random letters and numbers. The serial numbers embedded in the bar codes. Seven women dead and mutilated. Eight, assuming tonight's wasn't on the list.

Who was the synthetic? The cop part of me immediately identified him as the primary suspect, despite the fact that, so far as I knew, a synthetic shouldn't have been *able* to commit a crime, even against another synthetic. But who else could have a list of victims? Still, something about the big synth as the perp didn't ring true. He hadn't acted like a psycho gloating over his kills. He had been far too calm, composed…purposeful. If all the names were synthetics, then the crimes probably wouldn't have even had a report filed, and certainly wouldn't have been followed up on. So why bring it to a cop? Why bring it to me?

There was only one possible explanation. He knew. Not just about the rumors, the label of "synth-sympathizer" that clung to me. That wouldn't have been enough to risk life and limb breaking into a cop's apartment. He must have known more, known about my purged records, known about the secrets locked away in my past. But how? No one should have been able to access those. Right. And no one but me should have been able to unlock the door to my apartment. Shit.

I slumped back in my chair, nursing the whiskey, reading the names one by one. I was too tired, too drained by the events of the day to really process those names, but I read them anyway, over and over again. One more kept sneaking into the litany in my head, though it appeared nowhere on the crumpled piece of paper.

Annabelle.

Chapter 4

The rising crescendo of Ravel's *Bolero* dragged me from my slumber. I sat slumped in the armchair in my living room, empty tumbler dangling from my fingers. A nagging pain from my neck and shoulders reminded me that I was getting too damn old to sleep in anything other than a comfortable bed without paying a hefty price for it later. Ravel's twining melody kept sounding, playing throughout the speakers built into the apartment. A light flashed next to the wall screen as well. I probably looked like hammered hell, but I said, "Answer," anyway.

The music stopped at once, and the screen lit. On it, a young woman wearing a light blue lab coat over particolored scrubs stared back at me. She was of Asian descent, Japanese, or maybe Korean, with jet-black hair and almond-shaped eyes. High cheekbones watched over surprisingly full lips that were, at the moment, pulled down into a frown. "Detective Campbell?" She spoke in a low, furry contralto, and I heard the tiredness in her voice. And the doubt.

I set the tumbler on the coffee table—right next to my gun and the half-emptied bottle of whiskey. I scrubbed my hands over my face and then over my head, hoping to both wake up and make myself ever so slightly more presentable. The woman just stared at me, frown firmly in place and a faint air of disapproval settling in her eyes. She was young, late twenties, and, under the rumpled, unflattering clothing and fatigue, quite pretty.

"Yeah," I said, and the word came out a barely understandable growl. I coughed, to clear the sleep from my voice. I wanted to pour about three fingers into the glass and toss that back, but this call looked at least semiofficial so I refrained. "Yeah," I said again. "I'm Campbell." And, because I felt like I had to say *something*, I added, "Sorry. It was kind of a late night."

That got me a sympathetic twitch of the lips that could not, quite, be called a smile. "Of course," the woman said.

"And you are?" I asked, letting a little bit of the frustration from the case and last night's unexpected visitor creep into my voice. She had called me, after all.

A faint flush suffused her face at my words, and I realized that she was probably even younger than my first assessment. "Oh. Um. Sorry. It was kind of a late night." I got a real smile as she gave my words back to me, and it lit up her face like a sunrise, washing away the fatigue and crinkling her eyes in a way that had me wishing she was a few years older. But I was too damn old to keep up with twenty-year-olds, however pretty, so I just smiled a bit in return and waited.

She fumbled with a tablet for a moment, looking down at it and, I realized, struggling to regain her composure. When she looked up again, the blush was gone, and replaced by a mask of cold professionalism. "My name is Tia Morita. I work for Dr. Fitzpatrick."

I sat bolt upright, tiredness forgotten, and leaned forward, staring at the screen. The movement must have startled Ms. Morita, as she seemed to flinch back from her own screen. "You're the assistant the doctor assigned to my case? To the synthetic?" Part of me was eager for answers, another part running the numbers on Tia Morita. If she was truly in her early twenties, she certainly had not yet completed, and maybe not even entered, medical school. If Fitzpatrick had pawned off the "mule" on a flunky with no chance of finding anything out, I'd wring his scrawny little neck.

"That's correct, Detective Campbell," she said slowly and calmly. Too calmly. She spoke the way you would to try to calm an unfamiliar dog. One that looked ready to bite.

I drew a steadying breath, and eased back in my chair, forcing a tired smile onto my face. "Late night," I said again by way of apology, and she nodded in understanding. "What can you tell me?"

Her eyes flicked back to the tablet, and I realized that this was probably the first time she had ever been responsible for giving information relevant to an investigation to the police. An intimidating notion under the best of circumstances, and these weren't the best of circumstances. I scrubbed at my face again, and gave her a genuine smile.

"Take it slow, Ms. Morita. It's just you and me here. I assume you called me first, as soon as you were done?" Her chin bobbed in the barest of nods, eyes still locked on the tablet. "Good. Then think of this as a trial run. No Dr. Fitzpatrick looking over your shoulder. Anything you forget or miss, you can always call me later." I grinned. "Maybe after both of us have had a little more sleep."

She looked up, smiling back at me. Then she drew a breath and started speaking, rattling off her report in clear, crisp bursts. "OK, Detective. Here's what I know so far. The body that the EMTs delivered is a synthetic that belonged to a company called Party Toys Incorporated." Her lips twisted into a little moue of disgust. "They are, as you might imagine, a service that provides synthetics of a certain type for rent to various business and individuals to...well..." She trailed off.

"You mean they're pimps," I said flatly.

"Well, I suppose. Though the term has certain connotations that I'm not sure apply to synthetics."

I grunted. "Trust me. A pimp's a pimp, regardless of who, or what, they're pimping. Go on."

"Right. Well, the synthetic was registered under the name Molly Cummings." Another blush crept up her cheeks as she said the name, and I fought back a snort. I didn't want to embarrass the girl—her innocence was kind of cute. Besides, the synthetic hadn't named herself, and had clearly been destined as a sex worker from the moment of her "birth." "That's all the information I could get from her tag, just her name and place of employment. Well, some other stuff, too. The facility she came from, the training facilities she attended, things like that, that are part of her features list before she was purchased by Party Toys."

I nodded. Synthetics weren't born in the traditional sense, but they didn't spring full grown from the vat, either. Their growth could only be rushed so far, to about the equivalent of a ten-year-old child, before they had to age naturally. Anything longer, and something in the brain chemistry started to break down, leaving the synthetics catatonic. It was also illegal to sell most synthetics before they were the age equivalent of fifteen years old. The reasons for that were darker, but could be summed up by saying that even the most indifferent of lawmakers didn't like to think about the kind of things that happened to synthetics happening to something that looked like a preteen.

But the manufacturers didn't let that time go to waste. Instead, they sent legions of little synthetics off to "training facilities." That all those things lawmakers didn't like to think about happening likely happened during the course of the synthetics' "schooling" didn't seem to matter to anyone.

"Send me that information," I said, thinking of the list of seven names. It was a long shot, but maybe there was a link, buried somewhere in their backgrounds. "What else?"

"She was dead before the...evisceration took place," Morita said, stumbling a little over "evisceration." Well, most people did, I supposed. "I can't say for sure what killed her. Too much is...missing. But I found an injection site on her neck, and her blood work showed unusually high levels of potassium."

"Which means?" I asked.

She shrugged, and glanced down at the pad once more. "Maybe nothing." She sighed. "I can't say conclusively, you understand. The evidence isn't there." The frown was back, pulling at her lips, and I heard the frustration mixed with apology in her voice.

"Yeah, I understand," I grunted. "If you go too far out on a limb, you may not pass Fitzpatrick's test. I get it. But part of the job is giving me your best guess." It wasn't, not really. I didn't like lying to the girl, but she knew—or at least suspected—something more.

Morita sighed, and looked up from her tablet. Dark shadows hung under her eyes and her face sagged in fatigue. "An injection of potassium chloride most likely," she said.

I frowned. "Isn't that a fertilizer?"

"It has medicinal uses as well. And nefarious ones. It's normally taken orally, but if injected into the system without the buffer that digestion provides...well, at high enough dosages, it will stop the heart faster than you can say the words." Her shoulders lifted in a short shrug. "You see it all the time in the vids—the perfect, undetectable murder weapon. Which, since I can't conclusively prove it was there, seems true enough in this case."

"Poisoned," I mused.

"Probably poisoned," Morita corrected. "No heart, liver, kidneys. Nothing I can test further. There's not even much in the way of blood, though fortunately we had enough to run some tests." She frowned a little at that and her voice dropped almost as if she didn't want anyone to overhear what she said next. "I'm not entirely sure I was supposed to run the blood tests," she admitted. "Dr. Fitzpatrick said to do whatever I wanted, but there are rules in place around synthetics."

"I appreciate it, Ms. Morita," I said. I felt a little flash of guilt at the thought that I might have inadvertently gotten the girl to do something that could land her in trouble. "Don't bother telling Dr. Fitzpatrick about the poisoning or the blood work. He'll just want to hear the stuff you can back up with hard evidence."

She shot me a grateful glance at that, and nodded.

"If you find anything else, call me." I offered a grin. "No matter what time it is."

She returned my grin with a wan smile and gave a half wave to the screen. It went black, leaving me, once more, alone in my apartment.

I needed to get up, get showered, and get into the precinct. There were other cases on my desk, murdered people that the city actually cared about. Less than in days past, to be sure, since the sanctioned murder of synthetics provided a release valve for the thrill killers and psychos, but there were still plenty of "crimes of passion" to go around. I couldn't be seen working too hard on the synthetic—on the Cummings—case. So long as no one told me *not* to work it, I could still operate under the auspices of the New Lyons Police Department. But that meant making sure that nobody at the precinct actually knew what I was doing. Just how in the hell was I supposed to manage that? I sighed and headed toward the bathroom, that question, and one other, rattling around in my head.

Who was the strange synthetic that had broken into my apartment last night?

Chapter 5

The Forty-Third Precinct sat on the border between the red-light district and the warehouse district. At different points in New Lyons' damp and moldering past, the building had been pressed into service as a bank, an office building, and, briefly, an underground casino and brothel. Back when that kind of thing was not only illegal, but also not staffed with an endless parade of synthetics. My desk sat off to the far side of the open bullpen, symbolically removed from the beating heart of the precinct.

Once upon a time, robbery and homicide would have held the place of honor, the hub around which the rest of the department turned. Now, cybercrimes took center stage, staffed with cops who were more hackers than they were investigators, bent, even now, over their consoles, hard at work tracking black hats across the net. I had nothing against them—they were good cops, whatever their skill set, and by the official numbers, cybercrimes far outstripped violent crime and murder put together. The official numbers didn't include crimes against synthetics, of course.

I made my way to my desk and slumped into the faux-leather chair. Between Ms. Morita and the synthetic that had broken into my apartment, I had a list of murdered synthetics and the name of a company. Not much to go on, but I fired up the computer and got to work anyway.

I started with Party Toys Inc. There was only so far I could go without a warrant, and I had no chance in hell of getting one for an investigation around a synthetic, but they were a publicly traded company, so I pulled their financials. I was a long way from a financial genius—my talents lay in other directions, most of which were learned fighting wars, not doing long division—but I didn't need to be one to do an analysis. All I had to do was feed the file into our forensic accounting analyzer software, and wait.

While the program was crunching the numbers, I turned my attention to PTI's net presence, digging into their web pages, finding them on various social media sites, identifying employees who had public profiles. The amount of data readily available, if one cared to look, was staggering. I gathered the URLs, user names, everything else I could find and fed them into another forensic program, this one designed to do data mining and text analysis. It would crawl the web, searching through the various known pages and identifying other linkages, analyzing posts on social media, and hunting for anything suspect hiding in cyberspace, all without ever once going into anyone's system or looking at any private data, building a relationship map that outlined even the most tenuous of connections. I added a few more parameters: the names from the list the synthetic had given me, the cross streets where Ms. Cummings had been found, a few keywords around murder, disemboweling, poisoning, and anything to do with synthetics. After a moment's pondering, I added the phrases "sewer rat" and "albino" to the mix.

But I wasn't done yet. I pulled a data chip from my pocket and slipped it into my system's card reader. A list of files popped up, each a string of unique alphanumeric characters ending in a date range. I clicked on one of the files, and a window opened on my screen, split into four separate views of my building. One showed the front door, another the back entrance, a third the hallway leading to my door, and the fourth a view that mirrored the peephole on my apartment door.

I chose to live in a bad neighborhood, but I wasn't stupid. A little surveillance went a long way when it came to security, and though my building had no system of its own, one of the first things I'd done on moving in was convince the superintendent to let me install one. Given that it would cost him nothing, and he could market it to his tenants, it hadn't been a very hard sell.

Most of the time, I didn't bother looking at the footage. Despite the poverty around me, the majority of the crime stayed on the street, and people were more or less safe in their homes. I had no desire to spy on my neighbors. Not only was it none of my business, but if I knew too much, it might create a professional duty to do something about it. Few people liked having a cop around the building...most just barely tolerated it. If I started busting people for minor bullshit, that tolerance would turn quickly to hate. And then the walks home at night would lose all their charm.

But any doubts I might have had about the need behind the video surveillance had evaporated last night when I walked into my home to find a stranger in my chair.

I scanned through videos at ten times regular speed, watching a steady stream of people moving in and around the building, despite the late hour. The first file, the one that overlapped the time I returned to my apartment, did not show a large, pale, bald synthetic at any point. I worked backward from there, and with each new file I opened, my sense of trepidation grew.

Had the synthetic managed to avoid my cameras entirely? Or had he arrived at my apartment so early that I hadn't yet found him in the footage?

I had worked my way backward to the file covering eight to nine o'clock, a full five hours before I returned home and not long after I got the call about the eviscerated girl. At last, I found him. A khaki raincoat stretched taut over his massive shoulders, and a matching fedora hid his baldness, but there was no mistaking his fireplug build or his pale, almost translucent skin. He entered through the front door, timing his approach so that, without the slightest sign of hesitation, he hit the stairs a few steps behind another tenant, catching the door with a casual hand before it could swing closed and latch again.

I lost him in the building, but picked him up again when he walked onto my floor. He moved at a sedate pace. Nothing furtive or scheming about him—just a normal guy coming home from work. I watched, with morbid curiosity, as the synth walked up to my door and placed his palm against the lock.

That lock was coded for me, and *only* me. Nobody else was in the system, not even the landlord. I paid him extra rent to keep him out. The door should not have opened to any hand but mine.

But it did. Without hesitation. The synthetic put his hand on the pad, and waltzed into my apartment. "Son of a bitch," I muttered.

I ground my teeth and clicked on the part of the window that showed the peephole view.

It expanded to fill the entire screen, giving me a good, if distorted, view of the synthetic's face. The video program had a filter to fix the distortion, and I applied it to the best frame I could find. The resulting image was almost perfect. The synthetic was looking down—at the palm pad, probably—and his hat obscured everything from his eyebrows up, but I got what I needed. There were enough points in that picture for facial recognition to go to work. With luck, I would find an ID somewhere, in some manufacturer's records. But even without it, I could start searching the web of cameras around New Lyons and see if he showed up again. Or, rather, the computers could.

There were tens of thousands, maybe hundreds of thousands, of cameras scattered across the landscape of New Lyons. Old traffic cameras—largely useless since the advent of automated vehicles—had been repurposed to serve as "public safety" cameras, no longer aimed solely at the roadways, but actively panning and searching for trouble. Security cameras covered the approaches to all city- and federal-owned buildings. Retail shops, bars, and finance centers all employed security cameras as a matter of course and, in an affront to privacy everywhere, most gladly gave the NLPD access to their exterior feeds, in the hope that it would move them to the front of the line if they ever needed our help. Pick a company, and odds were good that they had electronic eyes upon you, eyes that someone, somewhere, could access and review.

My mother—who still taught psychology and philosophy courses at LSU—called it the "modern panopticon," stealing the term from nineteenth-century theoretical prison design where the inmates could all be watched by a single guard. A lot of her work centered on how the idea of being constantly observed affected the psyche and the myriad neuroses that could spring from it.

Well, New Lyons hadn't—quite—achieved a true panopticon. There were still a few blank spots in the city where the prying eyes didn't reach. And a good number of the cameras were on private networks not subject to intrusion by the auspices of the New Lyons Police Department. But still, if the synthetic was anywhere within the city, the odds of finding him were very, very good.

With the computer doing the heavy lifting, I turned my attention to the other cases I was working. There wasn't much. I had just closed a domestic violence case that ended in death, and the feds had swooped in and picked up a triple homicide that I had been working. That one had been industrial espionage gone wrong; the targeting corporation dealt with sensitive government contracts, so there was no way the federal government was going to leave the job to the locals. The feds had let me do all the grunt work to build the case, and then taken it from me with a smile and a "Thanks for the support. You have the thanks of a grateful nation." That and a fiver could get me a coffee.

That left just one—an apparently homeless man who had been beaten to death on the docks. It was a rare occurrence, not only because that kind of brutality most often flowed toward synthetics, who couldn't fight back and couldn't press charges, but also because they were, usually, easy to solve. But I didn't have a lot of hope in this case. Whoever had done it had either known where the eyes in the sky were or had gotten very, very lucky. Either way, they had kept everything firmly off camera. The crime scene technicians hadn't found any meaningful physical evidence—which was unusual in a beating case; normally there was at least some DNA transfer involved. But whoever had done it had done it clean. Uniforms had canvassed the docks, and, of course, no one saw or heard anything. The case was going cold fast, and unless a new lead sprang up, I wasn't going to make much progress.

And that was it. One case recently closed, one taken by the feds, and one where the bad guy was probably going to get away with it. The only new thing on my desk was the eviscerated synthetic from last night. I had to write a report for that one, and as a murder investigation, all I could do was flag it "case closed."

Instead of doing that, I changed the file code, reclassifying it from murder to felony criminal mischief. Synthetics were expensive, after all, and if anyone other than the rightful owner had killed the girl, a crime had still been committed. It was sophistry, and without a formal complaint filed by the owner, whoever that might be, it wasn't something I should be "wasting" my time on.

Eight dead girls, and nobody cared. How many synthetics died every year? I realized that I had no idea. It was a number I should know.

It was a number the whole world should know.

Chapter 6

I stretched my arms over my head and unleashed a yawn as I watched the computer continue to churn through the parameters I had set for the various forensics programs. It would likely be hours yet before they returned any meaningful results, and I had just sent off the last bit of paperwork of the morning. No new cases had come in. I was officially out of work to do.

I pushed my chair back from my desk and stood, continuing to stretch. It felt good after a short night spent sleeping in a chair—a comfortable chair, but still a far cry from an actual bed. I felt something low in my spine release with an audible pop that chased a moment of visceral worry with a feeling of relaxing warmth. I sighed and dropped my arms back down by my sides.

"Hey, Campbell." I wanted to curse as I heard the whining edge of that voice, but I managed to keep my tongue in check. I turned and found myself facing a group of four other cops. Fortier, the one whose voice made me want to swear, was a pudgy, sweaty troll of a man. A cheap suit hung poorly from his hunched shoulders, and as he moved, I caught sight of the dark circles of sweat staining the shirt beneath. His face was close and pinched, rodent-like but without even the charm of the meanest sewer rat ever to crawl from the shit and darkness.

There was a reason for the cheap suit, of course. Rumor had it, every dollar he had ever earned had been spent buying not one, not two, but three synthetics, all high-end toys. That thought was enough to make my skin crawl by itself, but Fortier was also one of those who bought in wholesale to the idea that I was a synth-sympathizer. And somewhere along the line, he had decided it was his job to give me shit about it. Not surprising, given his own proclivities, but annoying nonetheless.

Normally, I met his petty comments with a flat stare. He was such a little weasel of a man that that was all it took, most days. But today he was not alone. I recognized two of the three other officers with him. One was Robert Stevens, a decent enough guy most of the time, but young and, from what the rumors said, he spent way too much time down in the red-light district, spending his hard-earned salary with reckless abandon. Maybe he was supporting Fortier in an attempt to get some free time playing with Fortier's toys. It didn't seem too likely; Fortier didn't strike me as the type to share.

The other officer I recognized was Melinda Hernandez. Petite, dark hair, early forties, Hernandez was a hard-nosed cop who worked Guns and Gangs. She was also one of the few people at NLPD that I considered a friend. She stood a little apart from the other three, shadowing them. I could just make out the faint echo of worry deep in her slightly tilted eyes. There was a warning in those eyes, but something else as well. If I didn't know better, I'd think it was encouragement. Or maybe the better word was hunger.

The final officer was young, fresh-out-of-the-academy young. He looked like a rookie, but with a set to his shoulders and jaw that belied that moniker. Actually, he looked like two, or maybe three, rookies. He stood a towering six foot three, and had to be carrying at least 240 pounds of lean muscle. A regulation crew cut sat over eyes that bored into me, giving me his best championship fight weigh-in stare-down. He didn't wear a uniform. Instead, he wore a loose-fitting T-shirt and a pair of nylon shorts. In short, he was one scary bastard, and he was dressed to kick the shit out of someone—me presumably—in an NLPD-sanctioned fashion.

So, I did the one thing that was sure to piss the towering giant off. I ignored him, and smiled at Fortier.

"What do you want, Fortier?"

"You look like you could use some exercise."

"Of the two of us, I'm pretty sure everyone in the department could say which looked like they needed to get some exercise."

Something only distantly related to a smile stretched Fortier's lips. "Oh, don't worry, soldier boy. I get plenty of workouts at home. Lots of cardio." He made a crude motion with his hips that made me want to throw up in my mouth a little. "You know, I've been doing some digging around. Something about you always was a little off. I found some anomalies in your records. There were a lot of words like 'redacted' and 'expunged' floating around. Wonder why that is?"

The thought of *Francois fucking Fortier* digging his greasy fingers into my files brought a snarl to my face. The last thing I needed was the fat little fuck prying too hard at the edges of my juvenile records. Sure, they had been expunged, but my stint in the military told me just how much *that* was worth. I couldn't have Fortier digging too deep. My hands curled into fists, but Hernandez gave a little shake of her head.

I could take Fortier out in about half a second, even with Stevens and the rookie goon at his side. But no matter how much the squalling bastard deserved an ass kicking, if I handed him one, it would mean a suspension at the very least. And, probably, a couple of weeks without pay. I forced a deep breath and unclenched my fists.

"Fortier, the only secret around here is who you blew to make detective. Smart money's on the commissioner, but I figure even he wouldn't give you a pass. I'm guessing you had to blow all the way up to the mayor." Hernandez snorted and even Stevens cracked a faint smile. The goon just continued giving me his best impersonation of a thousand-yard stare. Easy to see where this one was headed, but I suddenly found myself welcoming it. "But if you want some exercise, I'd be happy to go down to the gym and beat a few dozen pounds of stupid off of you."

Fortier just smiled, a smug little smile that I would have *loved* to wipe off his face. With my boot. "That so, soldier boy? Well, I'm not really looking for any exercise—but my new friend here"—he gestured to the giant by his side—"heard somewhere that you were some kind of hot shit when it came to...what do you call it? Sparring? Hand-to-hand? Whatever bullshit play fighting you do." His smile took on a harder cast, and I felt a stirring in the pit of my stomach.

When I had been seventeen, like most teenagers, I'd been completely certain I could "handle myself" in a fight. Not that I'd ever actually been in one, not until Annabelle. But, horrors of that night aside, I *had* taken on two-to-one odds, and come out the other end relatively unscathed. The human mind is a strange wasteland, and despite the nightmares that plagued me to this day, I also walked away from that house with the belief that I was some kind of martial arts savant.

The military had quickly and brutally disabused me of that notion. My close quarters combat instructors had taken me apart with an ease that would have been crushingly embarrassing—if the "workouts" had left me any capacity to feel anything other than the pain of strained muscles and contusions. As the bruises healed, I discovered something about myself—I loved the thrill of physical confrontation. I loved the artistry and brutality of the techniques. I didn't enjoy inflicting pain on my opponents, or receiving it for that matter, but I did enjoy the sense of confidence that came from knowing I could defend myself at need.

For the most part, my reputation as a fighter stayed within a small community in the department—those who, themselves, were interested in learning martial arts, either for enhanced self-defense or to help them in the furtherance of their chosen career, or for the pure enjoyment of the art. While one might expect that *every* officer would seek out such training, one would be very sadly mistaken. Firearms, Tasers, and pepper spray were the weapons of choice, and the firing ranges saw much more use than the training mats.

"Unless, of course," Fortier said with a sneer, "you're scared or something? Maybe we can find you a nice docile synthetic to spar with instead."

Hernandez stepped forward and placed a hand on my arm. I couldn't quite tell if it was meant to be comforting or restraining, but it did remind me to release the breath that I had drawn in a long-suffering sigh. Despite having been born and raised in New Lyons, Hernandez spoke with a slight Mexican accent as she said, "You don't have anything to prove to these *pendejos*."

The words were conciliatory, but I could see the fire smoldering in her dark eyes. Hernandez was one of those who *did* seek out additional hand-to-hand training. We'd been on the mats together, and she had some idea of what I could do. I smiled at her, a real smile this time. "Thanks, Mel, but maybe some exercise *would* be a good idea. Take my mind off things." Not that I had anything against the rookie, despite the Friday Night Fights stare-down look he was still giving me, but if I let Fortier pass on this one, I'd never hear the end of it. Not from anyone that mattered, but the rumor mill already had enough of my grist to grind. And if he saw—really saw—what I could do, maybe it would discourage him from digging deeper into my records.

I winked at the big guy and gave Fortier my shit-eatingest grin. "After you, Francis."

* * * *

The basement of the precinct was divided up into a set of locker rooms, a firing range, and a gym. Most of the gym was dedicated to weight machines and treadmills, not unlike what you'd find in any fitness center in the country, but nearly a third of it had been set aside for hand-to-hand training. A variety of bags hung from the rafters, and mats covered the floor. There was no formal ring or cage, just white circles that stood out prominently against the blue backdrop of the mats. I stood within one of the circles, wearing gi pants and a loose-fitting T-shirt. The rookie—I still didn't know his name—kept his shorts and tee. We both had donned shin protectors and pulled on three-ounce MMA-style gloves.

A crowd had formed around us, some people who had been working the mats, others drifting over from the weights and cardio equipment. I heard the low buzz of excitement coursing through them, and did my best to ignore it. Some fighters like to get wound up, to feed on the onlookers or their own anger, to get their adrenaline surging before the first blows fell.

I preferred to be calm, relaxed. Fluid. Anger and adrenaline might make you throw harder, but it also made you stiff. It coerced you to attack when you shouldn't, and prevented you from backing off when that was the right move. So I took a long, calming breath and did my best to forget about the watchers, forget that Francois Fortier had set this whole thing up, forget everything else and just focus on the fight and the opponent before me.

The bell—really an electric chime—sounded, and we both dropped into our fighting stances. He went with a left lead, right hand hugging his right cheek, left extended before him, elbows tight. Classic boxer-style striker. His knees were slightly bent, and though his shoulders were mostly square, he set his hips with the lead hip turned slightly toward me. That was pretty common for practitioners who had started in tae kwon do and then moved on to other arts. He'd be a powerful kicker, maybe not quite as fast as most TKD guys, not at his size, but with his muscle mass any kick that landed could end it.

I crouched low, sitting deep into my stance, finding my balance and center. I matched him lead for lead, though I was just as comfortable with a right lead as a left. My hand positions mirrored his own, only I pushed my right hand out a little farther and I kept my hands open and loose. I had a strong suspicion he'd come wading in, throwing hard and heavy, so my initial play would be defensive.

We both shuffled forward, meeting in the middle of the ring. I extended my left hand, making a fist, and he touched gloves with me. Then we both sprang back, popping our hands back up. He moved well, keeping his knees bent, staying on the balls of his feet. And he was quick, especially for his size. I saw just how quick as he turned into a side stance, brought his trailing foot up to his lead in a quick shuffle, and snapped out a straight-legged side-thrust kick that, had it landed, would probably have sent me careening into the spectators.

But it didn't land. As soon as he'd turned his hip, I angled off line, pivoting out of the way as I let him pass. I ended up with me behind him, and I snapped out a kick of my own, knee turned outward, using the flat of my foot to stomp down into the back of the knee of his base leg. At the same time, my left hand shot out, hooking his left shoulder and pulling backward. The two opposite vectors of motion—pushing one way at his knee and pulling the other way at his shoulder—proved too much for his balance, and he toppled to the mats.

I could have followed it up with a ground and pound, but I didn't know enough about my opponent yet, so instead, I pivoted away from his fall, keeping my hands up and making sure to stay safely out of range of his lashing feet. I was glad I had chosen the more cautious course, since he hit the ground and immediately rolled, coming to his feet in a smooth motion that spoke of years of either jujitsu or aikido. I guessed jujitsu, probably Brazilian, and decided right then that I didn't want to try to grapple with the behemoth. My own ground game was decent, but it wasn't my best set of techniques, and I didn't want to take on someone twice my size who was as least as well trained.

He came at me hard, throwing a series of fast punches. Heavy, but controlled, each snapped out and pulled back again with a precision that belied the fury darkening his face. I parried and slipped for all I was worth, throwing an occasional counterpunch. Those were quick, short jabs, a few of which got through, but it was like punching a slab of granite. They didn't even slow him down.

I let him move me around the mats, giving ground slowly, holding myself in the transitory range that was too close for kicking, too far for knees, elbows, or grappling, forcing him to rely on pure pugilism. It bought me time, a few seconds, and it had the expected effect of feeding his anger. No one liked a target that refused to be hit. If he couldn't get through my defenses, he really had only two choices: step back and kick, or lunge forward and grapple. He elected to kick.

His lead foot pivoted back, and his right leg shot out, unleashing the power of his heavily muscled hips and legs. I didn't try to move away from it this time. Instead, I shuffled forward, bringing my left knee up and striking toward his kick in a counter that had been taught to me by a Pinoy. My knee caught his kicking leg in the meat of the inner thigh, and I stepped through and down with that leg. The half block, half strike had the combined effect of charley-horsing his kicking leg, and taking his balance as I crashed into him. But I didn't stop there.

My left hand lashed out in concert with my knee, catching and trapping his guarding hand. I pulled down and across his body as my foot hit the ground, turning his back to me and forcing him into a half bow, exposing the back of his neck. My right elbow swept high, coming down in a Muay Thai–style strike.

Had I landed that blow fully, it would have been a knockout. It also would have had a high chance of causing some long-lasting damage, given that the target was all neck and spine. I pulled the blow, hitting just hard enough that he knew—had to know—that the strike *could* have ended the fight, but soft enough that no lasting damage would be done. Even so, it was still enough that he dropped to one knee with a pain-filled grunt.

I dropped out of my fighting stance and put one hand on his shoulder. "You OK?" I muttered around my mouthpiece, offering the other hand to help him up, but eying him warily. I had dropped my hands, but not my guard—I figured there was a fifty-fifty chance that, enraged or maybe just a dick, he'd take another shot at me.

He spat out his mouthpiece, catching it in one glove and taking my proffered hand with the other. I didn't so much pull him to his feet as I provided some leverage for him to pull himself up. There was no way I could have moved that much mass with one arm. "Jesus," he said as he stood, rubbing at the back of his neck. It was the first word he'd spoken since the whole thing started. His voice was a rather pleasing tenor, surprisingly calm and almost rueful. "I'd heard you were good, but Jesus. No one's beaten me that easy in years."

I grinned as I removed my own mouthpiece. "You should have gone for the grapple. Things might have gone differently."

"The fuck?" Fortier demanded, pushing his way through the crowd. "I thought you were supposed to be good, Thompson." It was almost comical, watching the sweaty little troll glaring at the giant who, I had no doubt at all, could rend him limb from limb if he so chose. But given the performance the guy—Thompson, I supposed—had just given, I wasn't about to watch him get berated by the little asshole who was, if in rank only, his superior officer.

"Tell you what, Fortier," I said with a wry smile. "If you don't think he's all that good, why don't you put on a pair of gloves and see for yourself? I'm sure all these people"—I waved one hand at the throng of onlookers who were still watching intently and hoping the show would continue—"would just *love* to see that." A mutter went through the crowd that was part encouragement and part…hunger. Fortier paled a little.

"This isn't over, Campbell," he snarled. He turned and pushed through the people to make his way out of the gym, a somewhat bashful-looking Stevens in tow.

"What was that about?" Thompson asked as he pulled off his gloves.

I shrugged. "He's a dick." I glanced at the digital clock on the gym wall. Close enough to lunchtime, and I knew the computer would still be churning. "I'm going to get some lunch. You want to know more, you can come along. What about you, Hernandez?"

"In," she said simply.

Chapter 7

I enjoyed a leisurely lunch with Hernandez and the recruit, who, it turned out, had the unfortunate name of Thomas "Tommy" Thompson. He and Hernandez did most of the talking, chatting amiably about the force, New Lyons, and mixed martial arts. Neither of them mentioned Francois Fortier and his abortive attempt to have Thompson beat me into the ground. It felt good to unwind, to let the mysteries of the murdered synthetics slip away, if only for a little while.

As we were wrapping up, the big man, voice tentative, asked, "What was all that Fortier was saying about expunged records and redacted documents, Detective? If you don't mind my asking, that is?"

Hernandez went still with the question, and I knew it was on her mind, too. There was a part of me—a very small part—that wanted to come clean, to lay out the whole thing. But no. Maybe I could tell Hernandez, someday. But I'd just met the rookie, and I wasn't about to lay out my darkest secrets just because he seemed like a good kid. Still, I couldn't say nothing, either. So I told a small part of the truth.

"My military records have a lot of sections that have been redacted," I said, trying to keep my voice nonchalant. "I saw a fair bit of action overseas, and...well, let's just say I participated in some operations that weren't for the consumption of the general public. As a result, there are a lot of holes in my records. Fortier can read into them whatever he wants—he's a snake who likes pushing people's buttons. Don't let him drag you into his bullshit."

Hopefully Thompson wouldn't pick up on the fact that I'd only mentioned the redacted records, and not the ones that had been expunged. He just nodded affably. But Hernandez...she kept looking at me, and I could see the question lingering in her eyes.

* * * *

The digital readout on my phone read after 4:00 p.m. when, at last, back at the precinct, the computer issued an innocuous little chirrup.

It startled me from a reverie that was at least half doze, and I struck the mouse with more force than necessary. The facial recognition software was still going, searching for the mysterious synthetic across the city. That was a little surprising. The NLPD didn't have access to every camera that was live on the streets of New Lyons, but we had access to enough. Moreover, the cameras were distributed, not evenly, but in little clusters, all throughout the city. For someone, anyone, to not show up at any point meant they either lived a *very* localized life in one of the "blank" spots… or they knew enough about where the coverage was to avoid it.

I remembered the casual way the synthetic had bypassed my security, and figured it was the latter. I canceled the search. If it hadn't found him yet, it wasn't going to, and I could use the processing power elsewhere. The other searches—the cross-referencing of all things PTI and the listing of identifying codes from the victims—however, had yielded results.

I stared at the data, my lips turning down in a frown. Three of the eight girls killed—seven from the albino synthetic's list and the one from the case I'd caught—had been property at one time or another of Party Toys Inc. The search algorithm found them in the tax records of the company. Two of the girls first showed on the most recent tax return, listed only by serial number, on a table titled "lost or stolen" equipment. They showed in prior years as well, under "depreciating assets," again listed under nothing but the number. I tracked them back through the years, four for A73RM8932MC, the victim I knew as Molly Cummings, and six for Q93CC721AR. That serial number corresponded to one Anita Richards on the crumpled sheet of paper my favorite home invader had given me. They each would have been the equivalent of sixteen-year-olds when purchased. Molly died at twenty, Anita at twenty-two. An image of another girl, young and smiling at me, sprang unbidden to my mind. I ground my teeth and forced my attention back to the screen.

The records for the third girl started ten years ago, when she, too, had been listed, number only, on a "lost or stolen" form. There were only fifteen years of tax returns on record, and the third girl, E22KU683PS, Pamela Starr, had "depreciated" through all the years on record until she, too, was "lost or stolen." I had no way of extrapolating her age, at least thirty-one… A slight shudder ran through me as I wondered what happened, what *would have* happened, to these women had they not met an untimely end. What happened when their asset value depreciated to the point of zero? What happened as they aged and were no longer sought after by Party Toys' customers? Were they sold off to other companies or individuals, finding new life and labors? Or were they simply...destroyed? Put down like a horse with a broken leg? Tossed away like an outdated computer? What about the other synthetics, those that worked dangerous, backbreaking jobs specifically because the risk of injury was so high for a normal person? What happened when the inevitable injury struck? I had never considered it. Perhaps I had never *allowed* myself to, because, deep down, I knew the answer.

I couldn't undo those deaths, any more than I could bring Annabelle back. But I could at least try to find out why. Why had these eight girls died? No. That was only part of the question. What was it the albino synthetic had said... Why had the girls been mutilated? Why was the most recent victim, and presumably all the others, left in the street?

I grabbed my forty-five from my desk drawer and clipped the paddle holster to my belt. I confirmed the data transfer to my screen then slid it into a pocket and grabbed my keys. Party Toys Inc. had a local office, and if I hurried, I could probably catch someone there before they closed for the night.

Chapter 8

Party Toys Inc. sat in a downtown high-rise with a view overlooking the river. It wasn't the best piece of real estate in the city, but it was also a long way from the worst. Business, it seemed, was good. The lobby boasted faux-marble columns and floors sheathed in the same material. Various sculptures, either original work or excellent reproductions, sat nestled in alcoves or displayed prominently in the open, though cordoned off by red velvet ropes. Classical music played over the speakers, filling the chamber with a cascade of tinkling notes. The entire effect should have made me think of an art museum, but I found it crass and gaudy. Maybe if I'd been here to see a lawyer or an accountant or something, I would have felt different. But I wasn't. I was here to talk to the good people of Party Toys Incorporated. At best, you could call them an "escort service," but I wasn't feeling particularly charitable at that moment.

A uniformed security guard sat behind a tall desk—also sheathed in the fake marble—his eyes latching onto me immediately as I entered. I saw those eyes narrow as I approached, focusing on the bulge at my hip where my jacket covered my sidearm. The security, at least, seemed to be better than the artwork. I flashed my badge as I approached. "NLPD," I said. "I'm looking for Party Toys Inc."

The guard made a show of studying my badge. Maybe he was just being thorough. In any event, he nodded, glanced at a screen, and said, "Twelfth floor. Second bank of elevators."

I nodded my thanks and strode to the indicated elevator, hitting the call button. After a moment, a bell chimed and a set of the shiny metal doors parted, disgorging a press of well-dressed men and women, chatting amicably among one another. I didn't see any synthetics. Hadn't seen any anywhere in the building. I imagined those responsible for the upkeep, cleaning, and maintenance of the facilities wouldn't go to work until after the "real" people left. Pushing that thought aside, I stepped into the empty elevator and hit the button for the twelfth floor. The doors closed, the floor lurched beneath me, and the car ascended.

When the doors opened once more, I had to wonder if I was even in the same building, much less on the right floor. If the lobby below had been gaudy and trying too hard to impress, stepping onto the twelfth floor was like stepping into an ultramodern picture of elegance. Everything was sharp lines and contrasting colors, deep blacks and blinding whites juxtaposed to draw the eye and trick the brain into adding depth that wasn't actually there. The elevator opened into another lobby of sorts, facing a receptionist desk that seemed almost to float on impossibly thin metal legs of chromed steel. The chair behind the desk was itself an odd contraption, unforgiving angles giving way abruptly to sweeping curves. It looked like some sort of modern art, designed for show and not for use. It looked uncomfortable as hell.

The woman seated in it matched the chair perfectly. She had a slender, willowy body but with sweeping curves of her own, enunciating a femininity that the almost airy desk did nothing to hide. She wore a facsimile of a businesswoman's suit—skirt, blouse, jacket—but all the garments were tailored not just to enhance the curves of her body, but to accentuate, to draw the eye. Nothing about them was crude in cut or length, yet they somehow...promised. Lush black hair, so dark as to be almost blue, rolled from her head and down her shoulders, contrasting her ivory skin. Her eyes were a liquid green that bordered on the edge of blue, without ever crossing over, and her lips, plump and red and ever-so-slightly pouty, curved into a warm and welcoming smile as she caught sight of me.

She was a synthetic.

But if you looked deeper into that face, into those pale green eyes, the hardness lurking beneath the warmth and beauty emerged. Yes, the chair and its occupant were perfect analogies for one another. Like it, she was a showpiece, as much a work of modern art as a thing to be used. I had no doubt that hiding beneath the waves of onyx hair, the skin of her neck was raised in a scannable pattern that marked her as a synthetic. I had no doubt that her serial number would appear on a table of depreciation somewhere in Party Toys' tax records.

"How may I help you, sir?" the synthetic nearly purred.

I flashed my badge again. "I need to speak with someone in charge."

"One moment, sir. If you'd like to take a seat, someone will be with you shortly." She smiled as she said it, and put just the faintest hint of an emphasis on the words "with you," turning them into a languid promise.

I moved to the chairs, but remained standing. Something in the receptionist's words—the contrast between their soft innuendo and the edge that lurked just beneath her carefully trained expressions—filled me with unease. If synthetics were programmed to behave a certain way, here at least, was one that had not succumbed to it. She said, and I presumed *did*, all the right things, but still that edge lingered. It didn't detract from her beauty, but it did set it on a level that was somehow dangerous and unobtainable, like a jagged mountain peak. I shuddered to think of the kind of person that would request the "services" of a synthetic like her. I didn't think it would be the affable mountain climber who thrived on challenge. No. It would be the asshole who sought to dominate and subjugate all around him; who, seeing the jagged beauty of the distant mountain, would want to tear it down, and leave behind a broken shadow.

I trembled again, but this time it stemmed from an anger boiling deep within my gut. What would happen to you if your existence was simply to be hired out to an endless succession of such people, to be subject to their every whim? I knew from personal experience that such people existed, and it made my fingers twitch, itching to wrap around a throat and throttle the life out of someone. I clenched them tight, opened them, clenched them, taking slow, deep breaths as I did so, fighting to control the rage that had started boiling within me.

When it finally passed, I couldn't stop the relieved sigh from escaping my lips. I hadn't felt that level of anger in years, not since Annabelle. My time in the military had given me leashes with which to harness that anger and had taught me how to channel the rage into...something else. Call it controlled violence, but where the control was every bit as important as the violence.

I looked up from my reverie to see that I had drawn the attention of the receptionist. She was watching me—no, she was *studying* me—in that way women have, giving me the kind of look that convinced me that not only could she read my mind and tell me my shirt size, but also what I had for breakfast that morning. But then she smiled, a very different smile from the professionally sultry one that had greeted me when the elevator doors opened.

"Ms. Anderson will see you, now," she said. "Please, follow me."

I did so, making a point to keep my eyes where they belonged and not focused on the exaggerated, rhythmic swaying of her hips. We passed through a glass door and into a lushly carpeted hall. The hall branched off in four directions, but I didn't have much of a chance to look around, as the synthetic kept a brisk pace. I got a general impression of understated wealth. The office space would not have been out of place for a thousand-dollar-an-hour law firm. The hallways had an almost museum-like stillness about them.

I was escorted—no pun intended—to one of the few open doors. A wooden plaque on the outside read Sylvia Anderson, but there was no title or role printed there. I wasn't sure what to expect as the receptionist, all hard edges under velvet again, said, "A Detective Campbell to see you, ma'am." My mind's eye could not shake the picture of a debonair Old West madam running the local cathouse next door to the saloon.

Instead, I got a trim, middle-aged businesswoman in a suit that probably cost more than everything I owned put together. She stood from behind her desk, a massive thing of dark mahogany that had been polished to such a sheen that it seemed to give off a soft light of its own. She offered me yet another false smile and reached out to shake my hand. Her skin was three shades lighter than the desk itself, her hair short, straight, and jet black. Her grip was firm, quick, and practiced, like that of someone who frequently made handshake deals. "What can I do for you, Detective?" she asked, dismissing the synthetic with a flicking motion of her wrist. "Assuming, that is, you're not here for *our* business."

The smile took on a slightly wicked cast, but I didn't sense any real malice in it. Fortier was proof enough that establishments like this received customers from law enforcement, and why not? Nothing about the operation was illegal. For that matter, prostitution among non-synthetics had been legalized decades ago, and only dropped off when the people involved found it hard to measure up with the synthetic competition.

Voluntary prostitution didn't bother me—but the synthetics were chattels, property to be bought and sold, used and discarded, with no choice or say in the matter.

I felt the leashes of my anger slipping.

"Are you all right, Detective?"

Ms. Anderson had sat back behind her desk, and I realized I had been standing there, silent and, probably, glaring, for a few heartbeats too long. I forced a smile onto my face. "Sorry. I was thinking about a case."

"I understand," she said, waving me to one of the visitor's chairs before her desk.

I dropped into one. The upholstery felt like genuine leather, and the chair seemed almost to embrace me as I sank into it. Hell, it was more comfortable than my recliner at home, and I *slept* there more often than not. "To answer your question, I am here on business, but my kind, not yours." I pushed false cheer into my voice and looked around the office appreciatively. "I think you guys are a little out of my price range."

Another professional smile flashed across her lips in polite acknowledgment of my quip. "You'd be surprised. Our business model is built on selling cheaply to many. It's a largely renewable resource, after all." Her casualness made my skin crawl, but I fought to keep the revulsion from my face. She steepled her long fingers, resting her chin just on their tips. "Now," she said brusquely, "what can I do for you?"

I reached into my inner jacket pocket and pulled out a data disc. "There are the codes to three synthetics on this, all listed by your company as lost or stolen property. I'd like to know the last few clients each of them saw."

The smile vanished, replaced at once by an emotionless mask. It was a look I'd seen before, on every prosecutor and defense attorney whose path I had crossed. I immediately upgraded my estimation of Ms. Anderson. "We value our customers' privacy, Detective. I'm sure you understand that discretion is an important part of our business. I don't suppose you have a warrant?"

I fought back a sigh.

"No, Ms. Anderson," I admitted. "I don't have a warrant. Truth be told, I'm pretty sure I couldn't get a warrant to get this information. You see, the three codes on that list…all three of them have turned up dead."

She nodded, unsurprised. "It happens, sometimes. But we're insured against the damages, and, in the long run, it's better for our business if we work with the insurance companies rather than going after our clients. I'm sure you understand." She made as if to stand, words and gesture a clear dismissal, but I held up a hand to forestall her.

"I do understand," I said as sincerely as I could manage. "But these are unusual circumstances. Please, take a look at these." Also from my inside pocket, I removed a stack of four-by-six photos, printouts from Ms. Morita's preliminary report. They showed the evisceration in stark detail, under brilliant illumination, and from multiple angles. Ms. Anderson flipped through the photos quickly, making a slight gagging sound before sliding them back to me.

"I think we're done here," she said. The professional mask was gone, replaced with a frown of anger. And judging from the tightness around her lips, that anger was the only thing holding back the vomit. Good. "And why you think a bunch of post-autopsy photos would make me want to help you…" She trailed off, looking sick.

"You misunderstand me, Ms. Anderson. Those photos were taken *before* the autopsy. That's the state in which we found..." I almost said "the victim" but changed it to "your property." I picked the pictures up from the desk and tucked them back into my jacket, without looking. I'd already seen them more than often enough.

"Disturbing, I know," I continued, looking her directly in the eyes. "And I'm sorry for having to show them to you, but I need you to understand the...unusual nature of this case. You see, we're fairly certain the synthetic was still alive at the time the...mutilation...took place." A lie, but I needed information, and if that meant misleading this woman, then so be it. "We have three synthetics from your company found in this state, but we've uncovered eight in total."

I drew a deep breath and let it out as a slow, long-suffering sigh. "Whoever is doing this, they're increasing the frequency of the attacks." I wasn't 100 percent sure if that was true. It was difficult to establish a meaningful trend with only three points of data. "I'm afraid," I continued, letting some false resignation and very real frustration into my voice, "that this kind of escalation normally indicates someone who is getting ready to move on from synthetics to human targets. We see it sometimes, in serial killings, this...practice, I suppose is the only word for it, on synthetics. In a bygone era, they generally started on animals." I shook my head. "Now it's synthetics first, then on to people."

I went silent for a long moment, giving Ms. Anderson time to consider the implications of that statement. Then, I said, "You know, just once, I'd like to catch one of these guys before he started cutting up people. We've got enough dead synthetics—none of which belonged to the perp—to send him away for a long time...but only if we catch him. Still, I understand your position." I gave her a small, sad smile, and pushed myself up from the chair. Time for the final shot. "Thank you for your time, Ms. Anderson. I'll be back with a warrant, when the first mutilated human corpse shows up. Given how this one is going"—I shrugged—"I don't expect it to be too much longer."

I turned and started for the door. I hadn't made it more than a single step before she said, "Wait." There was doubt and turmoil in that single syllable, but it made me smile; then I immediately felt dirty.

I turned back to her, letting the very real hope welling in my chest show on my face, masking the disgust I felt for both of us. "Yes?"

"If I give you the information, can you keep Party Toys out of it?"

"Of course," I replied. "There's no requirement for us to disclose where we got our leads. As far as anyone has to know, it could have been off of extensive net research or a confidential informant somewhere."

She hesitated, doubt flashing across her face once more, but finally said, "Give me your contact info. I'll look into it and if I find anything meaningful, I will send you the information."

I knew it was the best I was going to get. I fished a card from my pocket, printed neatly with my name, screen number, and department e-mail address. So far as I knew, law enforcement officers were among the last people to use the anachronistic paper cards, but, technology aside, it was still the fastest way to give someone your contact information. "Thank you," I said sincerely. "You may be saving lives." Probably not the lives of anything she considered to be "real" people, but lives, nonetheless.

"You'll have everything I can find in the next couple of hours," she said. Her tone had shifted, going back to the confidence that had first greeted me, and underlain with another hint of dismissal. I took my cue, and offered my hand again. She shook it, briefly, and I made my way from her office. I had no real idea where I was. The corridors around me all looked the same, an elegant maze of dimly lit halls and firmly shut doors. I turned to the right and started walking. Before I could wander too far, the receptionist appeared, summoned, as if by magic.

Whatever ground I had gained earlier had clearly been lost, since she was once again steel beneath silk, her face set in a professionally disinterested smile. "This way, Detective."

I once more followed her through the maze of corridors, again at that too-brisk pace that had me almost jogging to keep up. I wasn't quite sure how she managed that—she was long legged, to be sure, but I was taller, not saddled with heels, and not practically crossing one foot in front of the other with each step to elicit that impossible amount of hip sway. Yet no matter how I lengthened my stride, she seemed to stay a half a step ahead, with an indifferent ease. In short order, we found ourselves back at the elevator banks, where, without a word, she pressed the Down button for me and then returned to her station behind the receptionist's desk.

The silence dragged at me, particularly since, for just one fleeting moment, I had seen a flicker of the girl behind the mask. I couldn't say exactly *why* it mattered to me, but suddenly it did matter very much, that this synthetic, this woman, see me as something other than one of the endless parade of people who saw her, and all her kind, as nothing more than things. As nothing more than the disposable toys the company letterhead so proudly decried. But how could I possibly convey that?

Without any preface or warning, I turned from the elevators, looked the receptionist in the eye, and asked, "What's your name?"

Three simple words, yet they shattered her mask as if it had been made of porcelain and the words themselves a sledgehammer. She sat there, a stunned expression obliterating all traces of edges and softness alike, revealing, perhaps for the first time, the person beneath the layers and masks and pain. In that moment, she ascended, at least in my eyes, to a level of beauty that far transcended the physical perfection that had been carefully engineered by the cold, symmetrical hand of science.

"My name is Sasha." she said, as matter-of-factly as I had asked the original question,

A question remained in her eyes, almost a challenge. I opened my mouth to speak but was interrupted by the loud, peremptory *ding* of the elevator. The doors opened with an electric buzz, and I realized that, like them, my mouth was hanging open. I wasn't sure what to say, wasn't sure how to process what had passed between us, so I shut my mouth with an audible snap, and nodded to the girl—to Sasha.

The doors began to close, and I stuck one arm out, intercepting them before they could. "It was nice to meet you, Sasha," I said at last, not able to muster anything more meaningful. As I stepped into the elevator and turned to watch her once more, I saw that it was enough. As the doors swept closed on the vision of her face, her large green eyes shone with the damp of unshed tears.

It was enough.

Chapter 9

I stopped and grabbed some dinner before heading back to the precinct, hitting the Pay button on my screen as my total rang up. The clerk behind the counter in the fast-food joint was a synthetic, and he stared at me with a blank smile and hooded eyes as he took my order. He wasn't particularly young, nor particularly old, maybe in his midthirties. I wondered, for a moment, how long he had worked behind that counter. There were no labor laws for synthetics. He could have been there since he was fifteen or so. People once thought that it would be robots and computers that took over all the low-skilled jobs and that the combination of world overpopulation and mass worker displacement would lead to either some sort of looming economic collapse or World War III. There'd certainly been enough war... at least in the third-world countries that served as proxies for the global powers. That might have stemmed global population some, but the truth was, in the first world, people had just stopped having large families, or, in some cases, any kids at all. Contraception was cheap and effective, and leisure was at an all-time high.

The past few decades had seen a decline in the population of North America and across most of Eurasia. Combine a culture less and less interested in having children with ever-tightening immigration controls and an aging population and the decline was inevitable. Throw into the mix the passage of the Basic Living Stipend, the guaranteed income for every citizen, and the pool of unskilled laborers dried up seemingly overnight. Automation was the first answer, but when Walton Biogenics started putting out the first synthetics, the "reliability, performance, and self-maintaining" features put the robots to shame.

Which left synthetics like the one taking my order to pick up the slack. For the rest of their lives. I tried to imagine twenty-five years of standing behind a counter, taking orders, washing dishes, with no hope for a better job, for career advancement, knowing that today was a repeat of yesterday, and tomorrow would be a repeat of today, on and on ad nauseam, ad infinitum.

Emboldened by my experience at Party Toys, I met the synthetic's eyes. "Thank you," I said as he handed over the brown paper bag. It was a courtesy that used to be reflex—still was when I dealt with people—but one that no one bothered giving a synthetic. You didn't thank a screen for connecting your call.

He tilted his head. "Is there a problem, sir?"

The words lacked any inflection, and his eyes stared through me.

"No. No problem," I replied. "I just..." Just what? Felt like saying thanks for getting my food? Felt like exercising some basic human decency. "Uh. Well. Never mind."

He didn't nod or acknowledge my words in any way, just kept staring past me, not looking at the next customer, who I could hear nervously shifting from foot to foot. Just staring at...nothing. I couldn't tell if I was making him uncomfortable—like I definitely was with the next person waiting to order—or if he really was so numb to basic interaction that his only response was a glass-eyed thousand-yard stare. "Well..." I gave a sort of half shrug and turned away, earning a glare from the middle-aged man with two brats in tow that was far more readable. I ignored it, my thoughts still on the synthetic.

Where did he go, when he wasn't here? For that matter, where did Sasha, the Party Toys receptionist, go? Did the "assets" of the company have a sort of barracks, perhaps hidden away somewhere on the premises of their respective owners? Did they have any amenities at all, or were they simply put away, like a coffeepot or a blender? How were their biological needs provided for? They had to eat something. I doubted they were getting home-cooked meals. Did they subsist on some sort of high-calorie protein bars? Or was it more like prison food? And, considered subhuman or not, there were waste products that had to be expelled. Once again, I was struck by how much I simply did not know about synthetics and how they lived. Perhaps, on some level, it was a subconscious choice to remain ignorant. But how much of it was societal? All of us, simply following some unspoken agreement to not ask too many questions about what was really going on, to not peer into the dark corners of our own utopia for fear of seeing the roaches scuttling for the shadows?

How could we have let it happen? That thought followed me all the way back to the station.

The precinct was still busy when I walked back through the doors—it was always busy. Even in the modern age, with violent crime at all-time historical lows and many vices of the past decriminalized, criminals never seemed to sleep; even most cyberattacks happened under the cover of darkness. As a result, my desk was only truly *my* desk when I was on duty—I shared it with another Homicide cop named Remi Laroche. He wasn't seated at it at the moment; maybe he was out on a call, or maybe he had gone to hit the gym. Regardless, I kept walking past the desk. Until my shift started tomorrow, it belonged to Laroche, and even though we shared the slot in the bullpen, it was one of the cardinal sins of the precinct to squat at someone else's desk.

Fortunately, the break room had everything I needed, which is to say, it had a comfortable couch where I could eat my burger and fries and it had wireless access to the precinct's network. I pulled my screen from my pocket while I took a bite from the burger, intending to check my e-mail and see if the inestimable Ms. Anderson from Party Toys Inc. had sent me the promised information. I didn't get the chance, however, as the screen started buzzing almost the moment I touched it. The unexpected ring startled me.

I managed to slap the device to my ear while simultaneously catching the burger before it experienced a tragic ending. "Yeah?" I muttered around a mouthful of what was, most likely, lab-grown beef substitute.

"Detective Campbell?" The voice on the other end of the line sounded uncertain, but I thought I recognized it. I racked my brain searching for the connection before remembering the call that had come in.... Had it only been this morning? I swallowed the half-chewed mouthful of food.

"Ms. Morita?" I asked in return, not sure if the voice on the other end belonged to the attractive—and far too young—lab assistant of Dr. Fitzpatrick.

A nervous laugh sounded from the other end of the phone. "It is you, then. Good. For a moment, I didn't recognize your voice."

"Sorry. You caught me with a mouthful of food." Despite myself, I hoped the sheepish admission would earn me another laugh.

Instead, I got a little gasp of embarrassment. "Oh. I'm so sorry. I can call back if you want?"

"No," I replied at once. Whatever the reason for the girl's call, I doubted it was social, and I needed any information I could get on the case. I followed the barked negative with an immediate "Sorry. You just caught me by surprise. I'm more than happy to talk to you, if you can stand the sound of a little chewing. What can I do for you, Ms. Morita?"

This time there was a long pause, long enough that I began to wonder if the call had dropped. I was just about to go through the whole "Are you there? Can you hear me?" routine when she spoke again, her voice softer, more hesitant than before. "I…I think I screwed something up, Detective."

It certainly wasn't what you wanted to hear from your medical examiner—even if your medical examiner was really only a half-trained assistant doing you a favor. I drew a slow breath. "It's OK," I said as reassuringly as I could muster. "Mistakes happen on every case. What did you find out?"

"I missed something obvious," she admitted. "Dr. Fitzpatrick insisted that it was time for the body to be destroyed—we needed the space, and there are some pretty stringent laws around the destruction of synthetics. Time frames that absolutely must be followed. You understand? But he did let me x-ray the deceased first, to see if I could get any further information from the bones."

I felt a slight sinking in my stomach as I realized her words meant the body, and any remaining evidence that might have been attached to it, were gone. Damn Fitzpatrick right to hell. I tried to keep the growing edge of anger from my voice as I said, "I assume the x-rays showed you something? Something you feel you should have found on the body?"

There was that hesitation again, and I could almost feel her gathering her courage. "Ms. Morita," I said again, then paused. "Tia, it really is OK. Unless you tell me you were somehow accidentally the killer yourself, I'm not going to get mad at you. OK?"

She sighed, a sound that mixed regret and just a trace of amusement. "OK, Detective. There was a shadow that showed up on the x-rays. I wasn't sure what it was, but it wasn't anything natural. No strange bone anomaly or genetic defect—not that those are even possible in synthetics. But whatever it was, it definitely looked man made. I took it to Dr. Fitzpatrick, and he informed me that it looked like a microchip of some sort. So, I did some research." Another long pause. "Detective…I think it was a tracking tag." Her voice dropped even lower, close to a whisper now. "As in GPS. Dr. Fitzpatrick informed me that it isn't an uncommon practice, particularly at the corporate level, to have synthetics chipped." She stopped talking, but I didn't step into the gap. I knew what was coming. "I found out too late," she finished in a rush. "The techs had already cremated the body. The chip was destroyed."

My brain was already churning. Would the chip have helped? Absolutely. Knowing the exact movements of the victim and the precise timeline of those movements would have been great. But we knew the body was moved after death, so it wouldn't necessarily give us the place where the murder happened. But it would definitely have helped. Would the information still be available? Tucked away on Party Toys' servers somewhere? And why hadn't the inestimable Ms. Anderson informed me of the fact that their synthetics were tagged? An oversight, or a deliberate omission? The problem with this entire investigation was too damn many questions and not enough answers to go around.

"Detective?" Ms. Morita said in a small voice.

"It's OK, Tia," I said, putting a smile that I didn't really feel on my face and hoping she could hear it in my voice. "It's not your fault. And while having that chip might have made things easier, there's no guarantee we could have gotten anything useful off of it, anyway. Besides, I've already made contact with the people at the victim's...employer...and they seem to be willing to cooperate. Now that I know about the chip, I might still be able to get the data from them." Not likely, but there was no sense in kicking the assistant medical examiner while she was down.

"So I didn't ruin your investigation?" The words were self-mocking, but I heard a hint of honest relief underlying them.

I smiled a real smile at that. "Not at all. In fact, you've been very helpful, and now that I know about the chip, I at least have something else to ask Party Toys for."

We made a few more minutes of polite small talk before I heard Fitzpatrick yelling something from the background. "You've got to go," I said, preempting her words. "I can hear the old Irish coot screaming from here." That earned me a quick, tinkling laugh. "If you think of anything else..."

"I'll call you," she assured me. We said our good-byes, and I hit the End Call button on the screen.

I finished my dinner in large bites, more interested than ever in the information that PTI was supposed to send. Would Ms. Anderson include the GPS data? My gut said no. Even though she seemed to want to do the right thing, corporations had an innate distrust of the police force. I couldn't really blame them. The Cyber Crimes Unit didn't spend a whole lot of time or effort on stolen credit cards or hacked corporate databases. They were more concerned with preventing and catching people who attacked the city infrastructure: camera networks, traffic lights, the power grid, that sort of thing.

When I was done, I used some of the paper napkins to scrape the grease from my fingers and tossed the trash into a nearby bin. Then I sat back on the couch and opened my e-mail on my screen. The program was smart enough to prioritize incoming messages based on what I'd done with previous e-mails. People I replied to often got pushed to the top, things I deleted got shunted off into a graveyard folder, and so forth. There was also a tab for new contacts. I swiped over to that one, and started scanning the e-mails. Only one jumped out at me. The subject was innocuous enough: *Info you requested*. The sender, however, was Sylvia Anderson.

I opened the e-mail. There was no salutation, no words wasted on greetings or explanations. I got a list of three rows and two columns. The leftmost column held the serial numbers of the three victims that had worked for Party Toys. The rightmost column, in turn, held three names, all different, all male: Thomas Caine, Jeremy Fowler, Robert Gutierrez.

I muttered a curse as I read them—Ms. Anderson had done exactly what she'd said she'd do…and not one millimeter more. I had no way of knowing if the names were even real or how many individuals they represented; they could be three different people, or three aliases of the same guy, or some combination thereof. She hadn't even bothered including dates. I could make some assumptions based on the dates of disappearance of the synthetics. Gutierrez had an "engagement" with the first disappearance from the PTI subset of missing synthetics, Caine the second, and Fowler with the most recent disappearance. It was more than I had a few minutes ago; not much, but better than nothing.

"Now what?" I asked the empty room. I could still access the station servers from my screen, even off duty, but triggering the search algorithms from the touch screen would be a nightmare. That would take hours, and I'd be better off going home and using my computer there. I could try calling PTI and asking for more information, but I had the feeling that the only way I'd get a single additional byte of data out of Ms. Anderson would be with a warrant.

I got up and peered into the bullpen. My desk was still open, but it would probably take fifteen or twenty minutes to enter the information, even from a keyboard. If Laroche came back to find me occupying his space, he'd be pissed, and rightly so. I could ask one of the other detectives, maybe even the Cyber guys, to run the info for me, and they would, but they would ask questions. Lots of freaking questions, and ones that I couldn't answer, not without revealing that I was pursuing an investigation that, at least in the department's eyes, should have been closed when I found out my victim was a synthetic.

I glanced at the clock on my screen. It was past seven o'clock, and my shift had ended at five. I was closing in on the twelve-hour mark, and I'd still be on call if anything came up while Laroche was otherwise occupied. Screw it. Tomorrow was another day; I would run the names then, from the comfort of my own desk, and see what could be found.

The journey back to Floattown passed quickly, my mind still churning over the list of names, and the questions the mysterious synthetic had left me. It was still early enough that my neighborhood had not fully converted from kids playing in the streets to thugs loitering on the corners, though I did automatically assume my "don't fuck with me" walk, as much out of instinct as out of any real need. Most of the neighborhood knew who I was and what I did, and I'd put down the first few challenges hard enough that it had been a long while since a new one had arisen.

My apartment building looked as unassuming as ever, though my previous evening's visitor had given me a newfound sense of paranoia. I needed to talk to my neighbors, to remind them to be vigilant about letting strangers into the building. I almost snorted at that thought. That's just what most of my fellow tenants would want—the pushy cop watching over their shoulders and telling them to be careful.

I made my way up the stairs, mind on the task of just how I was going to get the other tenants to listen to me. I found myself before my door, my feet taking me there on autopilot. Then my brain was jolted from its reverie by one simple observation.

The access pad by the door indicated that it was unlocked.

Chapter 10

"Son of a bitch," I muttered, staring at the unlocked door to my apartment—the door that I *knew* I had locked before leaving to go to work. Hell, the thing was set to lock automatically after five seconds, even if I forgot to lock it. It should have been locked, and no one should have been able to break that lock, though I knew the albino synthetic had already done so once before. It could be him; it was *probably* him, and if it was, he probably didn't mean me any harm. But that was two "probablys" too many. I slid my forty-five from its holster and took up a position on one side of the door. Then I grabbed the doorknob and pushed the door open, ducking my head and gun hand around the corner for a quick sweep of the room.

A hulking form once again sat, hands folded calmly in his lap, in my favorite chair. I had little doubt that the cameras would show, as they had last night, that he had been here for hours. I stepped into the room without a word, closing the door behind me. I swept the rest of the apartment, moving quickly from room to room, but making sure that we were alone. Only then did I holster my weapon and return to the living room.

Neither the synthetic, nor I, had said anything while I cleared my place.

I looked at him, taking in once more the bald pate, alabaster skin, and slightly pinkish eyes. A sardonic smile twisted his lips, but his body language spoke of a sort of ponderous patience, a willingness to sit and wait for the most opportune moment before doing…well, *anything*. There was something insect-like about that patience. No, not insect-like. Arachnid-like. A spider at the center of its web, just waiting for something to come ringing the dinner bell.

"Is this going to be a habit?" I grated. "Should I have a key made for you?"

"I don't need a key, Detective."

I snorted. "You've got balls. I'll give you that." I went to my kitchen and grabbed a tumbler from the cabinet. I dropped two ice cubes in it and poured three fingers of whiskey over top of them. I didn't offer the synthetic any, not because he was a synthetic, and not even because he had twice broken into my house. But the asshole was sitting in my favorite chair—that was inexcusable.

"What have you found?"

I took a small sip of the whiskey as I moved back into the living room, and, reluctantly, dropped down onto the couch. I propped my feet up on the coffee table, leaned back, and took another sip before answering. "I'm afraid I can't discuss ongoing investigations with people who make a habit of breaking and entering. The department has strict guidelines about that sort of thing, you understand." I tossed back the rest of the drink in one long pull and set the sweating glass down on the table. "What's your name, anyway? All day I've had to think of you as 'the albino synthetic who broke into my apartment.'"

He tilted his head slightly to one side, and the smile widened. "You don't like that, do you?"

"It's cumbersome. And not very precise."

"How many times do you think humans ask synthetics for their names?"

I sighed. Did we have to go through this again? Humans treated synthetics badly. Got it. I was probably even guilty of it myself, though, I hoped, to a much lesser degree. But I *was* the one working to stop synthetics from being murdered, mutilated, and deposited in the streets, and, oh by the way, risking my career and livelihood to do so. I really didn't want to have a long conversation about all the failings that could be laid at humanity's feet. There weren't enough hours in the day to even get up to the point where we were producing synthetics, much less to catalog all that had happened since. I didn't want to get into it; so instead, I asked, again, "Your name?"

"Silas." He said it with a slight sibilance, drawing out the *S* sound at the end. Something in the way he said it, in the narrowing of his eyes, told me that it wasn't the name he'd been given at the factory. It was his true identity, a name he had given himself, and probably something he had shared only with other synthetics.

I was once again struck by the notion that an entire subculture almost certainly existed among the synthetics, with their own norms and mores, and maybe even their own social hierarchy. The idea wasn't new—such subgroups had existed among human societies for ages, based on race, beliefs, and so forth. But the thought of a subculture among synthetics implied a degree of organization that made me slightly uneasy. That unease was balanced against an undeniable tingle of something that teetered perilously close to pride that the synthetic—that Silas—had just, however reluctantly, given me a glimpse into that clandestine world.

Which didn't change the fact that I was more than a little pissed at him for breaking into my house. So instead of dwelling too deeply on the thought of what the synthetics might be doing right under the noses of the rest of humanity, I said, "Well, Silas...what the hell do you want?"

"Justice."

His one-word response didn't surprise me, but it did make me grind my teeth in silent frustration. I wished he would stop talking in grandiose ideals, and get to the fucking point. Justice was a wonderful concept, but it was elusive and notoriously difficult to pin down. "We all want justice. We all fucking *deserve* justice. We seldom get it." I raised a placating hand before he could jump on that. "Though I will admit some get a hell of a lot more than others." I paused, but he said nothing. "So, what do you want from me?"

"I want you to investigate the deaths of those girls, and follow that investigation wherever it may go." He paused, but, given that I had just spent the entire day doing exactly that, I wasn't inclined to jump into the conversational gap, so it was my turn to sit in implacable silence. After a long moment, he spoke again, and it was as if the words were being dragged from him. "And I want you to stay alive long enough to see it to that end."

That got my attention. Sure, I chased murderers for a living, but outside of a very narrowly defined set of circumstances, most of them weren't truly dangerous. Within those circumstances, they would fight, kill, maim, do whatever they had to, but when faced with a man with a badge and a gun, they almost always folded. In the close to ten years I'd been a part of the New Lyons Police Department, I'd only fired my weapon once, at a perp who had been too high to recognize that he didn't have the training, much less the coordination or natural ability, to bring a knife to a gunfight and survive. I had been in a few other dangerous situations, though none to the degree where deadly force had been required. For the most part, the job had become routine, bordering on the edge of boring. The bulk of it centered around gathering evidence from crime scenes, talking to people while following up on leads, and waiting for lab results. But something in Silas's tone told me that he had specific dangers in mind, not just the generalities of being on the job, dangers that I definitely needed to know about.

And yet, he seemed reluctant to speak about it. If he kept this up, I was going to need to schedule a visit to the dentist. I forced myself to stop grinding my teeth, and took a slow, steadying breath. "Look, I just spent all day running down leads in this case. While, I might add, trying to keep the whole damn thing from the brass, since they'd happily shut me down, and shut me down hard, if they knew I was pursuing this. I'm tired. I'm frustrated. And I want nothing more than to grab another whiskey, then hit the shower, and the sack. But can I do that? No. Because, once again, I come home to find a stranger sitting in my apartment. In my favorite chair. So how about we drop the mystery routine, and you tell me whatever it is you have to tell me, then you go ahead and get the hell out of my house." I managed to get through it all without yelling, though my voice had crept up in volume.

His expression didn't so much as flicker, despite my rant. He still wore that same, slightly sardonic smile. "Very well, Detective. I wanted to see if you've made any progress, and also to warn you."

"I'm following some leads. I'm already in deep enough. I can't discuss the case with you. Department policy forbids it." I smiled as I said it, the polite, professional smile that was drilled into me at the academy. It was the nicest way I knew to say, "Fuck you."

He laughed. A rocking bass of a laugh that started near his belly and burst forth from his mouth. It startled me so much that my hand dropped instinctively to my sidearm. It took a full ten seconds—with the big synthetic laughing all the while—to get my heart rate back under control and register that there was no threat. "What's so goddamned funny?" I demanded, trying to steady my shaking hands as I reached for my glass. It was empty, so I slammed it back to the coffee table.

He raised one hand, as if to say, "Wait a moment," as he continued to laugh. When he had finally finished, red faced and nearly panting, he gasped, "Detective, you amaze me. Even when trying to display your anger, you treat me as more human than ninety-nine percent of your kind."

I didn't really know what to say. He must have seen my confusion, because he continued. "Telling me about your case no more violates any privacy or security guidelines in your department than telling your microwave would. Or perhaps, telling your dog would be a better analogy." I heard the faint trace of bitterness beneath the humor in Silas's voice, a bitterness that, I suspected, had been bottled up for many years, left to ferment, and distilled into a powerful and heady brew. "Synthetics are not covered under any privacy laws; we have no privacy of our own, of course, but neither are we considered a security risk." The sardonic half smile returned. "After all, who would share secrets with us?"

Something in his tone, in the smile, made me suspect that the answer to that question was damn near everyone. Synthetics were in our schools, babysat our children, cooked and cleaned in our homes. They even shared our beds. For most people they were a fairly constant presence, always around, but never really noticed. How much did they overhear while moving invisibly through the world that humans thought of as their own? How many secrets fell unwittingly into their grasp? If that collective knowledge could be pooled...

A slight shudder ran through me. If they ever did share those secrets, I suspected there was nothing that their community as a whole wouldn't be able to discover. I didn't begrudge them the knowledge, certainly, but information was one of the purest forms of power, and the synthetics might very well be sitting on a cache of it that could only be described as nuclear.

"So quickly, you grasp the situation," Silas said. "You see the potential when given only a glimpse."

"Right," I agreed, "I'm a magnificent specimen of humanity and a detective to the stars. So tell me again why I want to share any information with you? Particularly given the implications of your last statement?"

"Because I set you on this path."

Now *that* was certainly debatable. Sure, he'd given me some names to investigate, even given me some questions to consider, but I would have investigated last night's murder, regardless. But would it hurt to talk to him? What had I really learned in the past day? It might even help to discuss the details, to let my brain work in the background while laying it all out there for someone else. That was part of the reason cops had partners, after all. It could also earn me a little quid pro quo...and there *was* the second half of why he had said he was here: the warning.

I grunted my assent. "Fine. Only link I've been able to find among the victims so far, is that three of them worked for an outfit called Party Toys Inc., an...escort service, I guess." I didn't pause long enough at that for him to correct me. There were less flattering terms for places like Party Toys, but it wasn't relevant at this point, and we had a lot of ground to cover. "All three girls went out on calls, and never returned. Information on their final disposition never made it back to PTI, where they were, ultimately, listed as lost or stolen property." I paused. "I got the impression that PTI has a fair amount of 'lost and stolen property,'" I added. "Enough that these disappearances didn't seem like more than business as usual. Probably, at least a few a year."

Silas nodded. "It is common in the sex trade. Most of the men and women who engage in those services are just looking to spend time with one of the 'pretty people' without having to navigate the complicated social hurdles that you humans seem to put in place around sexual dalliance. Others... others are more...exotic in their desires. Violent. At times, fatal. We lose thousands, perhaps tens of thousands, of young synthetics every year to sexual violence."

I felt my lips turn down in a frown as thoughts of Annabelle once more danced through my brain. Well, that had certainly led to death, if not exactly the way Silas was implying. But I didn't doubt his numbers. I'd been a cop for nearly a decade, a good chunk of that in Homicide, and I could see the correlation between the rise in the availability of synthetics and the drop in the official homicide rate, even over that short time. I was too much the cop—which was the same as saying too much the cynic—to think that the reason was the better quality of life the synthetics supposedly provided the "real" humans. Synthetics screamed and begged and bled like the real thing; but if you killed one, you didn't get prosecuted for it. The murder-for-pleasure psychos and the more run-of-the-mill abusive assholes had found a judicial-system-approved way to get a pass.

"In any event," I continued, "I managed to get a list of the names of the last clients for the murdered girls. I'll run them in the morning, and then see where they lead."

Silas steepled his fingers in front of his face. "Very well, Detective. It seems like you are taking this seriously, after all, and making an active effort to pursue it."

That sent a little tingle of irritation running up and down my spine. "Of course I am," I growled. "I said I would, didn't I?"

"Yes. And I believed you to be different. But I've thought that of others before as well. There are many people out there who are sympathetic to the plight of the synthetics and the injustices visited upon us…right up until the point at which they are called upon to help." He dropped his hands to his knees and leaned forward, staring at me intently with those strange pink eyes. "At that point, when they must weigh the comfort and security of their current life against the possibility—or perhaps certainty—of ridicule and social isolation, most, almost all, choose to turn away from us, and to resume their lives as if nothing ever happened."

I snorted. "Yeah, well, I'm not too concerned about the complex social networks I've built, and as for the security of my life, it seems like people can waltz in and out of my place whenever the hell they want. So if you came all this way to warn me about that, you wasted your time."

"No, Detective. I came to tell you that, if you continue your investigation, people will most certainly try to kill you."

Chapter 11

Silas's words washed over me.

If you continue your investigation, people will most certainly try to kill you.

The words, or maybe it was the synthetic's flat, emotionless delivery of them, had a certain gravitas about them. There was nothing quite like coming to terms with the idea that someone out there wanted you dead. I had been to war and been shot at, wounded, returned fire, and taken lives. But that had been a very impersonal, almost professional, sort of killing on both sides. We'd been ideological enemies, sure, but no one had been looking for me, specifically, to track down and put a bullet into.

I *had* felt the chill of a nice, personal death wish once before, in that long-ago room with Annabelle, though I hadn't had the luxury of dwelling on it at the time. That night still haunted my dreams, and that personal animosity, of knowing another person wanted your heart on the proverbial platter more than anything else in the world, was no small part of those nightmares.

"Well," I said after a moment's consideration, "at least it won't be the first time."

That earned me an arched eyebrow from Silas. As it seemed like he was perfectly willing to revert back to nonverbal communication and since I had no desire to learn who was out to kill me through a rousing game of charades, I asked, "Would you care to shed a little more light on this death threat?"

Silas steepled his fingers once more and leaned back in the chair. "I cannot tell you much," he began.

"Bullshit," I interrupted, drawing another arched eyebrow. I was getting tired of the game, the mystery, the…well, the bullshit. "You can tell me plenty, certainly more than you've let on. If you actually want me to find out who's responsible for killing those girls and see them brought to justice like you claim, you'll tell me everything. No more games."

"I do not know everything, Detective," Silas said. "But I will tell you most of what I know."

"What do you mean, 'most'?" I demanded.

"I will not tell you all of it, Detective. I will tell you what I know that will help you find the killers, and keep you safe. But some of it…well, you would not believe me if I *did* tell you, and it would only cloud the issue. If that is not sufficient, then I will leave, and you will not hear from me again." He stopped speaking and regarded me with those disconcerting pink eyes.

I didn't like him deciding what I would or would not believe; not because he was a synthetic—I would have been equally pissed at *anyone* trying to tell me what to think. The irony, however, was not lost on me. My irritation at not getting everything I wanted seemed like a child's tantrum beside the literal programming and conditioning that synthetics, all synthetics, underwent. That conditioning didn't stop at limiting what they thought…for all intents and purposes, it told them exactly who and what to be. What had it cost those like Silas, who seemed to have broken through the brainwashing? How did his own people, those still locked into their programming, view him? Would he be the hero, or the villain? Were there others like him out there? Or was he the only one running around, telling everyone the emperor had no clothes?

I thought of Sasha at Party Toys Inc., of the hard, knowing look in her eyes that had nothing to do with the compliance and supplication that was supposed to be bred in the bone of the synthetics. No, he wasn't the only one. How many, then? How many of those staring, blank faces hid minds that had, somewhere along the line, fully awakened to the world around them? How many of those minds burned with hatred? How many hungered for revenge?

I couldn't be sure, but I thought that, had I been in Silas's position, my heart would be blackened by hate for the so-called humans who subjugated my people and doomed me to a life that I knew was so much less than it could be.

Silas still stared at me, waiting for me to decide if I could accept his limitations. I didn't like it, but I didn't have a choice. I had the distinct feeling that the synthetic could empathize with that, though. "Fine," I grunted. "Tell me what you can."

"Did you know there is only one company licensed to manufacture synthetics?" he asked by way of answer.

I did know that. Some of the first reading I had done during my stint in the military—when I had both the time and access to the net again—had been researching synthetics. My search had centered on how emotional attachments to synthetics could form, a desperate attempt at finding a coping mechanism in the wake of Annabelle's death, but it had taken me far and wide across the digital landscape. There were thousands, tens of thousands, possibly hundreds of thousands of articles, blog posts, research papers, religious musings, and more, all centered around the synthetics.

All written by "real" people, of course. I hadn't found a single byte of information that came from the proverbial horse's mouth, or from those who had taken the time to interview them directly.

Most of those articles were simplistic affirmations of what everyone already knew. Synthetics weren't real. They were subhuman. They were lesser beings, not even on par with animals because—at least according to some of the religious blogs—they were created by man and not the hand of God. But all those articles, whether they were mainstream acceptance of the treatment of Silas's kind or blistering denunciations buried in the deep web, all of them started at the same place.

"Walton Biogenics," I said in response to Silas's question.

"Yes," he nearly hissed. "Walton Biogenics. The only company allowed to manufacture synthetics. Do you know *why* that is the case? Why, in a supposed free-market economy, one company is granted a monopoly on what is, perhaps, the most lucrative 'product' ever created?"

"Tell me," I suggested.

"You understand that synthetics aren't really synthetic at all, not by the definition of the word. We are every bit as organic as the rest of humanity, with the same genetic makeup." Something that wasn't quite a smile twisted his lips. "Actually, we have a superior genetic makeup, the product of targeted genetic engineering to reduce certain traits and enhance others." His voice took on a note that was somewhere between bitter and proud. "Even those designed for construction or menial labor are not only stronger and faster than their human counterparts, we're also more resistant to cancer, have stronger immune systems, and a life expectancy longer than your own. Or we would, if so many of us weren't simply killed out of hand."

It took me a moment to digest that. I mean, yeah, one look at Silas and I knew he was stronger than me. With his compact frame, barrel-like chest, and bulging arm muscles he looked more closely related to a simian strain than a human one. And sure, most synthetics were prettier—by a long shot—than your average human. More bodily symmetry, better muscle tone, metabolisms that could give teenagers a run for their money. But resistant to cancer? Enhanced immune systems? Longer lives?

"If that's all true," I began, but Silas cut me off.

"Then why hasn't this wonderful technology been released to humans?" Silas asked, completing my thought. He stared at me for a long moment, his eyes searching. I began to wonder if the question wasn't meant to be rhetorical when Silas said simply, "Doing so would destroy your society."

The calm certainty in his words left me speechless. It wasn't just the casual declaration of the end of society as we knew it, but something about the way Silas spoke told me that he not only thought it inevitable, but, ultimately, longed for it.

I thought about that. Not just Silas's longing—the root cause of that seemed readily apparent. Synthetics were slaves, even if no one used the word. Were I in his place, I, too, would long for the end of the society that oppressed me, enslaved me, in the hopes that whatever rose from its ashes would be better for me and mine. It was human nature. And, that, I realized, was the rub. It was *human* nature. "The one thing that could bring about the fall of society as we know it, would be to convince everyone, beyond any reasonable doubt, that synthetics were human."

He leaned forward, eyes narrowing as he stared across the coffee table at me. "Exactly," he said, biting the word off.

Chapter 12

"I don't understand," I said, frowning in thought. "How would these genetic breakthroughs convince anyone of anything?"

A quick look of irritation flashed across Silas's face. "I get some of it," I said, letting a little irritation creep into my own voice. "If it was developed for synthetics but works on humans, that certainly suggests a...a relationship. But we've done medical experimentation on close genetic relatives of humans for centuries. We've adapted those results and used them, without caring whether the initial research came from chimps or rats or whatever, and certainly without suggesting that we are somehow the same as those animals."

"*We* are not the same as those animals," Silas snarled, and I heard real anger in his voice for perhaps the first time.

"I didn't mean..." I began, realizing that I had, albeit inadvertently, compared the synthetics to lab rats and monkeys.

"I know." He sighed, the anger draining from his face and leaving in its place a look of near-complete exhaustion. It was there for only a moment, hidden beneath the implacable mask so fast that I had to wonder if I'd seen it at all. "I know what you meant, Detective. Regardless, the sameness is verifiable in this instance."

I arched an eyebrow. "Then why hasn't it been verified?"

"Walton Biogenics holds all of the data, all of the patents, all of the intellectual property rights, everything about us wrapped in layers upon layers of legal protections. Did you know that it is illegal for most medical professionals to draw blood from a synthetic? Or to administer anything beyond the most superficial levels of care? Why do you think that is? Why do you think the bodies of synthetics are so promptly consigned to the crematoriums, even in cases where useful information might be learned from a more thorough examination?"

I thought of Ms. Morita and felt a flash of guilt. Had I made her an unwitting accomplice to a crime? "I don't know," I admitted. "I thought it had to do with—" I stopped, choking a bit on the words, but I had to say them. "With warranty issues."

"Yes," Silas snapped. "That's precisely what Walton Biogenics wants you to think. They're just the friendly local company, trying to do the right thing and stand by their product. The crushing press of corporate greed predates electricity, much less synthetics, and people still buy into the marketing schemes, turning a blind eye to the harm in exchange for an easier life." He shook his head in disgust. "The reason they offer such a wonderful 'warranty' is because they want to minimize the chances of any of their 'product' undergoing any genetic-type testing. In point of fact, they've used patents and copyright laws and an army of lobbyists and lawyers and bought-and-paid politicians to ensure that any such testing carries with it harsh legal penalties. Now, tell me why."

The anger was back. Silas was biting each word off, nearly coming up off his chair—off *my* chair—glaring at me with burning eyes. I felt my own anger flare in response, filling my chest with a tightness. Who was this guy to break into my house and berate me, when all I was doing was trying to help him? Didn't he realize that I wasn't the bad guy here?

But I was the guy who had done nothing to change the situation.

The anger drained from me, leaving in its wake a faint echo of shame. It wasn't pleasant, but it at least allowed me to focus on what he had actually said, and not the blame that I had heard. I thought about it, and no matter how many different twists and turns I let my mind wander down, I always came back to the same spot. "Because they're afraid of what that sort of genetic testing would reveal—that the synthetics, down to their very genome, are human."

"Yes."

I wanted to deny it. Wanted to shout that the government, that the *people*, wouldn't allow such a thing to happen, wouldn't stand idly by and permit such abuse. But I knew better. People—those who counted as "real" people, anyway—were living better than they ever had in human history. Part of that was the steady march of progress, but not all of it. According to the studies, there was a strong correlation between happiness and the ownership of synthetics. Who wouldn't be happier with a servant to do all the grunt work? And "servant" was only one of the many roles—and the least dark among them—that a synthetic could fill.

I nearly jumped from my seat as a rusty, almost painful sound emerged from Silas's mouth. It took me a moment to realize he was laughing again. Wherever that laughter came from, it was not a place of sunshine and rainbows, but somewhere dark and twisted and full of thorns. "You don't want to believe it, and yet you can see the truth of it, can't you, Detective? And you have already answered the question that most would ask: 'Why would we let this stand?' Because if you didn't, society as you know it would crumble, tearing the thin veneer of utopia from the cancerous ulcer that is the world you so reluctantly live within. Do you see now why Walton Biogenics would kill to keep their secrets safe? Do you see why the government that you served as a soldier and continue to serve as an officer of the law would turn a blind eye toward—or even encourage and assist—their actions?"

I did. And worse, I understood that this wasn't the kind of thing that could be kept from society at large unless most—hell, maybe *all*—of the country's leaders, at the federal, state, and even city levels, were in on it. The level of corruption, the willingness to allow for the subjugation of an entire people... I suppose it shouldn't have surprised me, but it did. Politics was a dirty game, sure, but it was a game that politicians played against each other, not one that they were supposed to be perpetrating on the people. It was hard to believe that not one person had come forward.

But then again, maybe they had tried...and maybe they had been stopped.

"So if Walton Biogenics knows I'm investigating, they're going to come after me. With what? Corporate hit squads?" I said it half-jokingly, but I knew guys from my service days who had gone on to work for private defense contractors, the kind of people who billed themselves as bodyguards and security forces but spent almost as much time fighting—and fomenting—wars in backwater countries for one warlord or demagogue after another. There wasn't much they wouldn't do, given a large enough paycheck and the chance to pull some triggers.

"Yes," Silas said, his voice dry and serious. "And I think you already know that." He stood then, gathering his hat and shrugging into his coat.

"Wait," I said, jumping to my feet. "You're going? But you've barely told me anything. What do these murders have to do with revealing that your people are...well, people? Why are these women being eviscerated? Do you have any proof that Walton Biogenics is behind the murders?"

Silas ignored me as he walked to the door and waved his hand in front of the screen. It responded to him as it would to me, unlocking the various bolts. He pulled the door open with one hand as he positioned his hat on his head with the other.

He threw one last glance over his shoulder. "Be careful, Detective. You have friends out there that you don't know, but the same holds true of your enemies. And if they don't know you yet, they soon will."

With that cryptic remark he left, leaving me to wonder two things. First, what the hell was that last remark supposed to mean? And, second, how had a synthetic—a synthetic!—overcome their programming to break into my apartment in the first place? If he could do that, what else could he do?

Chapter 13

I slept poorly and woke early, chased from sleep by visions of eviscerated women and faceless men in immaculate suits with stainless steel scalpels clutched firmly in their hands. A pale Silas, grown to impossible size, towered over us all, glowering down with a flat, disapproving expression plastered on his face, like a disappointed moon surveying the shambles we'd made of the earth. I couldn't shake that image, that thought that the man was silently judging me, and that, whatever it was he was expecting me to do, I was coming up short.

For some reason, that bothered me. It shouldn't have. I was doing everything I could to solve the murders, to find out who was behind the deaths. Hell, if I had understood Silas correctly, I was doing what I could to help pull down a society in which I held a fairly exalted position.

Maybe that was what was bothering me. I made a fairly stolid and unexciting rebel. I was a cop and a soldier—careers that instilled a sense of duty, responsibility and a deep respect for authority—and about as far from being an anarchist as a person could go. I didn't see myself as the guy who stood up against the government and society, and shouted endlessly about all the wrongs being perpetrated around me. And yet, I was about to go into work, to continue running a clandestine investigation, misusing government resources to uncover something that, once uncovered, could never be stuffed back in the darkness and, dramatic hyperbole aside, might very well result in the end of the world as we knew it.

Worst of all, as I stared blearily into the bathroom mirror, I couldn't say for sure if I was upset because I was pursuing this path, or if I was upset because it had taken me so damn long to take the first steps down it.

I scrubbed my hands over my face, then shook my head, trying to force the thoughts from it through sheer kinetic energy. I still had leads to run down, a faceless corporation hell bent on my destruction, and maybe a society to overthrow. It was going to be a busy day.

Time to get to work.

* * * *

I started with the computers.

It took a half hour to get the search running on the names Ms. Anderson had sent over. There was an art to effective searching, and it was an art that all cops—not just the Cyber guys—learned pretty damn quick. I spent that thirty minutes entering every piece of useful or related data I could think of into the search algorithm: the names, the dates of the disappearances of the Party Toys Inc. girls, the links to PTI itself, reentering the serial numbers, and, after a moment's hesitation, the ties to Walton Biogenics. Linking the megacorp to an investigation might raise some flags later down the line, but I figured I'd deal with that particular crisis when it arose.

"You're in early."

I turned to see Melinda Hernandez standing behind me. She had a fresh bruise forming over one eye, but wore a smile that would rival any wolf for its satisfied hunger.

"Sparring?" I asked, nodding at the eye.

"Nope," she said. "A cholo who thought beating on his gangbanging buddies meant he could take on a little girl." She said the last two words with great irony and greater relish.

"You didn't kill him, did you?" I asked it half-jokingly. Hernandez was fully capable of killing a man with her bare hands, but even if it was justified, it would look bad in the blogs. Cops had guns for a reason, after all.

"Nope," she said again. "Broken arm. Wouldn't have done that much, if the little bastard hadn't sucker punched me. He'll be OK, though." Her grin widened to something that would have made that wolf jealous. "His reputation, on the other hand…"

I chuckled. No matter how much we had progressed, some things never changed. Some guys' pride could never take the hit of being beaten by a "girl." Some of my better instructors had been women, and they'd taken great joy in showing the bigger meatheads in class that size and strength were no guarantee of victory.

"Why are you here so early?" she asked again. "I thought your shift didn't start until nine."

"Needed to get a data search going," I admitted.

Hernandez nodded. "Might take all day. Anything I could help with?" I thought about that. Hernandez was a good cop, and a genuine, caring person. I didn't know her stance on synthetics, or even if she had one. With my reputation, it was a topic I tried my best to avoid. How would she react if she knew I was pursuing a murder case that by definition wasn't murder? I could use her insight, though.

"The case is pretty sensitive," I hedged. She frowned. Cops weren't supposed to keep things from other cops. I sighed and went with tactful honesty. "Look, the brass probably wouldn't want me pursuing it, so I'm doing it on the sly. If word gets back to them…"

A fierce grin split her face. "The brass can kiss my ass," she said. "I got reamed pretty good by the captain for the broken arm thing, even though it was a clear case of self-defense and well within department guidelines." She gave a strange twitch of the lips that was somewhere between a grimace and a smile. "The cholo's already whining about excessive use of force."

"Generalities only," I said.

"Yeah, yeah." Hernandez waved a hand as if shooing away my conditions. "Shoot, already."

"OK. I've got a murder, a strange one."

"Didn't hear about it," Hernandez said. "Strange ones make the news."

This was the problem with working with cops. No matter how much they intended, even wanted, to listen to what you had to say, they had a habit of picking out every inconsistency, every nuance, to try to catch you in a lie. It was bread-and-butter stuff, an automatic reaction for anyone who made detective, but it was annoying as hell when they did it to you. I frowned at her and she chuckled.

"OK, OK. No interruptions, Detective. No interrogations. Carry on."

I snorted. "So, I have this murder, a strange one," I said again, glaring at her with mock anger. "A little digging, and a little outside help, and it looks like it might just be the tip of the iceberg."

"You talking a serial killer?" Hernandez—despite her earlier promise—interrupted. I couldn't blame her, not really. Synthetics, and the unique legalities surrounding them, hadn't had the same impact on serial killings that they had on other types of violent crime. Serial killers had their own psychosis and it demanded "real" human suffering. But confirmed serial killers had always been vanishingly rare, and any detective worth their salt wanted to be the officer to bring one to justice.

"I don't know," I admitted. "I don't think so, at least not in the way you mean. I'm thinking something more along the lines of corporate-sanctioned murder. Killing to keep your business secrets safe."

Hernandez nodded. "Wouldn't be the first time in history that a corp has shed blood for profit." She frowned thoughtfully. "That why you don't want the brass to know? You investigating a corporation that's in with the department?"

I could have lied to Hernandez then, and she would have accepted the lie. It was easy to think that an international company with their vastly deep pockets and questionable scruples would happily buy influence with politicians and law enforcement agencies the world over. It was easy to think that, because it happened every day. Hell, from what Silas had said, it had certainly happened as part of this case. Walton Biogenics had to be in bed with the government, which meant they had at least some influence over law enforcement. But that involvement wasn't why I was reluctant to let the details of the killings—the fact that no one but a few would consider the victims to *be* victims—come to the surface.

I had very few friends, on the force, or off it, and I wasn't going to risk Hernandez's friendship by lying to her. "No," I said simply. "I mean, there's a chance that the company involved has their hands in the precinct...but I haven't come up against that yet. There are other reasons, though." I didn't go into them, and for once, Hernandez didn't ask. So what could I tell her, really, that would give her enough information to offer her insights, but without dragging her in too deep...or confirming my synth-symp reputation?

"My murders have pointed back to a genetics company," I said. "I've got a source within the company..." Silas wasn't an employee of Walton Biogenics, but if they created him, I figured it wasn't too much of a lie to claim he was part of the company. "He tells me that they've discovered that some of their products are defective and might end up causing...let's call it, unexpected side effects." Like anarchy and chaos and the downfall of society as we knew it. But I left that part out. "Rather than issuing a general recall, the company has started identifying those who may have used the defective products and is...eliminating them."

Hernandez had gone from smiling to frowning to looking slightly disgusted as I spoke. "That's horrible," she said. "Innocent people being killed by a corporation because the corporation screwed up?" I wondered, briefly, if she would be as disgusted if she knew the dead were synthetics. I hoped so, but I still couldn't bring myself to tell her, to risk exposure. To risk the investigation being shut down. To risk losing a friend. "You sure you can't go to the brass about this?" she continued. "If there have been multiple murders, and if they're still doing it, you have to alert the city."

I shook my head. "I've got no real proof, Mel," I said. "The corporation in question ensured that the bodies were destroyed before any real evidence could be gathered from them. And it hasn't happened all at once. I've got eight confirmed deaths, but they're spread out over years."

"So, all you really have to go on is the word of one employee? And, I assume, he's not the most reputable of sorts." It wasn't a question, but I nodded anyway. "Not the most reputable" described Silas pretty well, and the fact that he was a synthetic would make him not only suspect in the eyes of most, but render any official statement completely useless.

"I've confirmed the deaths," I said. "These people all died or disappeared, and all in unusual circumstances. I've also got some names associated with the most recent deaths, people who I think might be the operators for the company in question. They all had contact with the deceased or missing at or around the times of death or disappearance. That's what I'm looking into now, places where these people—or maybe just one person, if the names are aliases for the same hitter—may have crossed paths with some of the victims."

"Trying to find more crime scenes," Hernandez said with a nod. She tilted her head slightly. "You're not telling me something, Campbell. What is it?"

I sighed. I knew Mel, and I knew that if I told her of Silas's warning, I was going to have a hard time getting rid of her. At the same time, she was a good cop, a good detective, and once she sniffed a lead, she wasn't going to let it go. I decided to come clean. "The guy, my source? Well, he came and saw me again last night. Gave me a sort of vague warning. Pretty much implied that if this company found out I was poking around the edges of their scheme, they wouldn't hesitate to have me killed."

"They'd take out a cop? And you believe him?"

I shrugged. "Most people wouldn't consider my source to be reliable at all, but yeah, I believe him."

Melinda frowned at me, and I saw her concern in the furrowing of her brow. "I don't suppose I can convince you to go to the captain?" she asked. She didn't bother waiting for a response—she knew me well enough that she knew that wasn't going to happen. "No, of course not. Look, *hermano*, investigating something off the books is one thing, but if it's going to get you killed..." She hesitated. "Are you absolutely sure there's something here?"

I was. I wasn't sure that Hernandez would see it that way, though. Still, I needed help, someone I could call on for backup if I thought I was walking into a tight situation. "I'm sure." I felt dirty as I said it. I wasn't lying, but I wasn't exactly telling her the whole truth, either.

"OK, Campbell." She gave me a hard, eager smile that said she wasn't going anywhere. "What can I do to help?"

Chapter 14

"I think I have something, Campbell."

I had given Hernandez the list of names that Party Toys had provided me. I already had my searches running, but the computer work was only part of the job of a detective. Melinda had a lot more friends on the force than I did, which meant she had a more extensive network of people willing to provide information. And with her work in Guns and Gangs, she had a much deeper pool of street informants as well. I hadn't really expected her to get results, though, not when looking into what I suspected were a bunch of corporate hit men.

"Already?" I tried to keep the note of surprise out of my voice. By the patronizing grin she gave me, I failed. "How?"

"I have my ways, Detective," she said with an air of mystery. "I have my ways."

I waited, but she wasn't going to make it easy. I sighed. "OK, Hernandez, we'll do it your way. What did you find out?"

She hitched one hip up on the corner of my desk and waved at my computer. "Open up your e-mail."

I did as ordered. There wasn't much there—no active cases meant no test results or inquiries coming in—but I did see an unread item from Hernandez. I opened it up. There was no body, just a link. I recognized it as a link to the secured server where surveillance footage was stored. I looked at her.

"Well," she encouraged. "Go on. Click it."

I clicked on the link, and a window popped open. The video was from a stationary camera, single point of view, directed at the front of what looked to be an old-fashioned barbershop. "What am I looking at?" I asked.

"This shop is owned by one Manny Santiago. We watch him for Guns and Gangs. He's sort of a shared resource that a lot of the gangs use. He's kind of an identity theft savant. Mostly electronic, but he can do old-school paper, too. He gets a lot of traffic from criminals wanting new identities after we get onto them and from illegal immigrants of all flavors."

"Why haven't you busted him yet?" I asked.

She grinned. "He's good, *mano*, but we're better. We tumbled onto him years ago, and sicced Cyber on him. We've penetrated his network, and we can pretty much keep tabs on every ID he cranks out. Mostly, we leave the small-time stuff alone, and only go after the big fish. Sure, it means some illegals get papers that maybe they shouldn't, and some misdemeanors go unprosecuted, but it gives us a way to keep tabs on the really bad guys." She grinned. "The hardest part is convincing the big bads that we found them some other way, so they don't green-light Manny and put him out of business the old-fashioned way."

I nodded. I didn't like it, but policing was always a tradeoff. More often than not, you leaned on the little fish until they gave up progressively bigger fish, promising their freedom in exchange for the next guy up the food chain. "What's he got to do with my case?"

"Keep watching."

The time-lapsed video had already shown a steady stream of customers going into and out of the barbershop. Almost all of them were black or Latino, with white faces few and far between. And regardless of the race, they all wore clothing associated with street culture. Which made the affluent-looking white male in an expensive suit who showed up after a few minutes stand out like the sorest of thumbs.

"Well, well, well. Who do we have here?" I wondered aloud.

"Don't know," Hernandez admitted. "I've got facial recognition running, but nothing so far." Her grin turned into a broader smile. "But I had Cyber check their logs on Manny. A couple of days before that guy shows up, guess who our boy Manny cooks up in his little computer lab?"

I shrugged. "Who?"

"Guy by the name of Jeremy Fowler. Only, the real Jeremy Fowler is an engineer that lives on the West Coast and had his identity stolen a couple of months ago."

Jeremy Fowler. The name immediately rang a bell. "Shit," I muttered. "Fowler's on my list. When was this video taken?"

"About a week ago."

Which would line up nicely with my timeline. Get a false identity. Plan out the killing. Maybe find a place to dump the body. Then contact Party

Toys to set up the meet. The mutilation was elaborate enough that it would probably take a few days to set up. Something about it was bugging me, though. "It's too neat," I said, at last. "Come again?"

"Look, I think there's a major—and I mean *major*—corporation behind all this. Why go to a two-bit crook and get a stolen identity? I'm pretty sure that they have the resources to create their own fake IDs. Why risk working with an outside man?"

"You sure it's this corporation, and not just some sicko?" Hernandez replied.

I thought of Silas, and the lengths he had gone to get into my apartment. It was possible—albeit extremely unlikely—that Silas had sold me a bill of goods. It was possible that he really was "defective product" and he was the one committing the murders. Identity theft didn't make this Fowler—or whatever his real name was—a killer, and showing up in Party Toys' client list wasn't a crime. It certainly wouldn't be the first time a serial killer tried to get close to, and even drive the investigation.

I considered it, mentally reviewing what I knew about the big synthetic. Silas was mentally capable of murder, synthetic programming notwithstanding; I had no doubt of that whatsoever. But would he be able to bring himself to brutalize and murder a fellow synthetic? And would his mental capability allow him to overcome the physical limitations imposed by his programming? On the first count, I didn't think so. I couldn't put my finger on it, but when he spoke about his own kind, there was something in his voice, an anger at how they'd been treated, yes, but also pain and something akin to reverence. Besides, much of what he told me rang true. Too much of it confirmed things I thought I had known since that day so many years ago. And the man on the video was definitely out of place; something about him set my detective sense tingling.

"No real evidence," I admitted. "Nothing solid, anyway. But my gut says we aren't talking lone wacko."

"Well," she said with a grin, "there's one way we can find out who this *pendejo* is and why he walked into that shop."

"Go and question Manny?" I suggested.

"Go and question Manny."

* * * *

Manny's Barber Shop wasn't exactly in the best part of town. It was a better area than Floattown, but not by much, and had the added unpleasantness of sitting in the shadow of one of the city's sewage treatment plants. The smell wasn't as bad as one might think—the city did make some effort to combat it, after all—but it was still a long way from pleasant. It was a little after noon as we rolled up on the place, the unmarked cruiser that Hernandez rated as part of Guns and Gangs looking out of place among the beaters and rust buckets that lined the streets here.

"Let me do the talking," she said as we exited the vehicle.

I just nodded. We were in gangland, and that wasn't my territory. She knew the scene much better than I did. This was Hernandez's show, and I was pretty much just along for the ride. I could live with that.

Stepping into the interior of the barbershop was like stepping back in time. There were four deluxe barber chairs, laid out in a neat row, and another line of simple plastic chairs for people to wait. All four of the barbershop chairs had people in them, each being tended by an actual, real-life human being—which is to say, none of them boasted the kind of symmetry of features or self-effacing mannerisms of synthetics. In fact, the barbers, two black men, one Latino man, and one Asian woman, were all engaged in boisterous conversation with their patrons and each other, lending the shop an almost festive air.

That conversation stopped as Hernandez and I entered the establishment. It's not like we were dressed in a way that screamed "cop," or anything. I was wearing a suit, sure. And, OK, maybe it was a little rumpled and on the cheap side. But apart from the wrinkles, the suit could have just as easily pegged me for a teacher or poorly paid and underappreciated law clerk. Hernandez, on the other hand, looked like her suit had been tailored for her, not bought off the discount rack like mine. It had a light and airy look about it that not only highlighted her fitness, but did a much better job of concealing her service weapon.

OK, so maybe Hernandez's clothes didn't scream cop...mine, on the other hand...

"I'm looking for Manny," Hernandez said.

"He's not here," the Asian woman replied at once.

Hernandez sighed. "Is that right. So, if I go into the back room there"— she nodded at a closed door—"I'm not going to find him?" She took a step in that direction, eyeing the woman as she did.

"You have no right to do that," the woman replied. "No warrant. Your business is not welcome here. You can leave now."

"Or what?" Hernandez asked. "You'll call the cops?" She smiled a sardonic little smile and took another step.

I almost winced at that, but I didn't interfere. Gangs was a different world from Homicide, and I knew that Hernandez couldn't afford to look weak out here on the street. I kept my mouth shut and did my best to look intimidating, staring hard at the patrons and the other barbers who had, so far, contented themselves with glowering at us.

From somewhere in the back came the sound of a door opening and then slamming shut.

Instinct kicked in and I was moving before my brain had a chance to catch up. Three quick strides took me to the door leading deeper into the barbershop, and I tore it open. There was a small office beyond it, but not the kind I would have expected to find in a barbershop. In my frenzied dash across the small space, I counted no fewer than seven computers, and a half dozen printers and magnetic strip writers of various kinds to boot. I didn't let that slow me down, though—I wasn't here to catch a forger.

I tore open the back door, which exited into an alleyway running north and south. A quick glance to the north showed nothing, but as I looked south I caught a glimpse of Manny—at least of a man the right height and build running from me at maximum speed. I took off after him, trying to keep my eyes a little beyond the fleeing form, so I didn't miss a twist or turn in his attempt to lose me.

I wasn't a runner. Hell, I *hated* running. The best thing about getting out of being a beat cop and into Robbery and Homicide was that I was no longer expected to go dashing pell-mell through streets and alleys in pursuit of suspects. But I still spent a lot of time on the mats, and even if I was no marathoner, I had plenty of endurance. The distance between me and Manny closed at a satisfying clip.

As I neared, I could see him throwing frantic glances over his shoulder every few steps, gauging how much I'd gained. Which is why he didn't see Hernandez dart out from between two buildings half a block ahead of him. Hernandez *was* a runner, and her lithe frame handled pounding the pavement far better than my bulk. She did this kind of thing—the running, not the chasing—for fun. Poor Manny had never stood a chance.

Hernandez was fairly petite. Manny was no heavyweight, but he probably had fifty pounds on the detective. She didn't try to stop him by main force. She didn't have to. As soon as Manny realized she was there, he did his best to dart around her. She let him pass, but flicked out one foot as he did so, catching the heel of his trailing leg. The foot she clipped clashed into Manny's other foot, and he stumbled and went down. Hard enough that the poor bastard slid face-first and then rolled once or twice along the pavement before coming to a groaning stop.

I was on him as soon as he stopped moving, flipping him onto his belly and slapping the cuffs on him before he had even regained his senses.

"Neat," I said to Hernandez between gasping breaths for air.

"Pretty routine," she replied. She wasn't even breathing hard. Couldn't she at least pretend to be winded?

A crowd had started to gather, curious citizens drawn by the commotion. This wasn't the kind of neighborhood where cops were welcomed with open arms, so we were getting a fair amount of hard stares and low mutters. And the inevitable array of recording devices. "Let's get Manny here back to his shop," I suggested.

"I didn't do anything, man!" Manny said, having apparently regained enough of his senses to start protesting his treatment.

"Then why did you run?" Hernandez asked, her tone disarmingly reasonable.

"I want a lawyer," was the man's reply.

If the forger clammed up on us, it would take weeks to get anything out of him. Not to mention blowing the sting that Guns and Gangs had running on his operation. Better cut that one off forthwith.

"Sure thing, Manny," I said. "If we take you in, you can bet that the very first thing we'll do is get you a lawyer. And that lawyer will do a wonderful job of advising you right up until the point that we throw your ass in jail for the next twenty years." I gave him a sort of considering look. Manny was in his early twenties, thin, and with features that were almost delicate. He tried to hide his fine bone structure behind a scruff of beard, but it had come in thin and patchy and, if anything, made him look even younger. "I don't think you're going to like the joint much, Manny." I shoved at his shoulder to get him turned and gave him a light push in the direction of his shop.

"Of course," Hernandez said, picking up the thread as we walked along, playing good cop to my bad, "you may not *have* to go to jail. We don't even have to take you in. This could all just be a big misunderstanding."

I couldn't see Manny's face since I was walking behind him, half propelling him back up the street toward his shop, but I could feel the tension in his body and sense his sudden interest. It seemed the kid was smart enough to know that hard time could be pretty damn hard indeed. "What do you mean?" he asked.

"We don't care about you, Manny," Hernandez said sweetly. "You're small time. Two bit. Not worth the paperwork. You understand." She made a flicking gesture, like brushing away an annoying gnat as we turned the corner and made it back to his shop. I pushed him—not too roughly— through the back door and into his office. I shoved him into a chair and leaned against one of the desks covered in various computer equipment. Hernandez shut the door behind us.

Manny was sweating now. Not just from the run, or from being collared. No, he was sweating because we had so casually invaded his most holy of holies. We were relaxing in his office, his sanctum, which was, unquestionably, full of all kinds of evidence that could put him away for a long time. "What do you want?" he asked, his voice hovering somewhere between hope and fear.

From what Hernandez had said, he worked for some pretty bad people. The kind of people who probably had lots of eyes in the neighborhood and likely knew already that their favorite forger was having a little talk with the police. Hernandez looked over at me. Guess it was my turn.

I pulled my screen from my pocket and unlocked it. A few quick swipes had the enhanced version of the shot of the mysterious Mr. Fowler exiting the barbershop. I held the display up in front of Manny's face. "We need to know who this guy is, where he is, anything you have on him."

Manny made a show of studying the picture for a minute. Then he shrugged. "Never seen him."

Hernandez smacked him—lightly—across the back of the head. "Come on, Manny. You don't expect us to believe that, do you? We photographed him coming out of your shop."

A clever little twinkle lit in Manny's eyes. "Maybe I wasn't here that day. Or maybe I was stuck working in the office. You know how it is, *chica.*"

I smiled to stop myself from grinding my teeth. Manny and his IDs were a lead, my first real lead, but if he was smart enough to stonewall us, there wasn't much I could do. I could only lean so far on him before I fell flat on my face.

"That's OK," Hernandez almost purred. "If you can't tell us, we'll go talk to Michael Gutierrez. And don't worry. I'll make sure to tell him Manny sent us. *Chico.*"

I didn't know who Michael Gutierrez was. It was clear, however, that Manny did. At the mention of that name, the blood drained from his face and a new sheen of sweat broke out on his forehead. I pulled Manny to his feet and turned him around. "Hey, what are you doing?" he demanded.

I pressed my thumb to the pad on his cuffs and they beeped, then clicked open. "Letting you go," I replied, tucking the cuffs back into their holder at the back of my belt. "Sounds like we don't need you, after all. We'll just go have a nice long chat with Mr. Gutierrez instead."

Hernandez was already walking to the back door, and I moved to follow her. "Wait," Manny exclaimed. "Just wait, OK? Maybe I did see that guy."

I stopped and turned back. "Jeremy Fowler," I said. Once more, Manny flinched back, as if from a blow.

"How do you know..." he started, but then trailed off again.

"Assume we know everything about your little operation, Manny," Hernandez said. "And assume that, for the most part, we don't give a damn. You can make your little fake IDs all you want. We don't care about forgers. We care about murderers. And that's what your Mr. Jeremy Fowler is shaping up to be."

As Hernandez spoke, Manny had gone even paler. "You...you know?"

"What, you think we thought all these computers were for balancing your books? You're not nearly as smart as you think, *ese*. Spill it, Manny," she said flatly. "Or we go have that little talk with your friend."

"OK, OK. I need to get to my computer."

That raised a few red flags. In Manny's shoes, I would certainly have some kind of kill switch baked into my gear to send it all into meltdown at the touch of a few keystrokes. But Hernandez didn't even flinch. "Just remember, Manny," she said, "nothing you do on those computers will save your ass if we go have that little conversation with Mr. Gutierrez."

He paused for a moment, his fingers hovering over the keys. Then, without a word, he began typing.

It only took a few seconds. "He paid me with a wire transfer," Manny said as his fingers flew over the keyboard. "I didn't ask his real name. Didn't care, you know? But sometimes people try to pay with bogus accounts or with..." He paused. "Let's say money that isn't properly cleaned, OK?" I snorted at that. "Yeah, well, I can't have an electronic trail leading back to me, you know?" Now that he was working, Manny seemed almost to forget that we were cops. I could see why Hernandez had referred to him as a savant. He didn't even seem to be paying attention to what he was doing. His fingers seemed to have a mind of their own, slamming down on the keys with abandon while he kept talking.

"So, I do some checking, you know? Follow up on the trail, make sure the money I'm getting paid is clean. And you know what?"

He seemed to be waiting for an answer, so I said, "It's clean."

"Squeaky clean, *mano*. Squeaky clean. Straight up *corporate* clean, if you know what I mean. The accounts traced back to a company called Translantic, a shipping company. That seemed weird, so I kept digging, you know? And it turns out, this Translantic is owned by another company, and *that* company is owned by a third company, on and on up through like a dozen different corporate entities. And do you know who all those companies traced back to?"

"Walton Biogenics," I said.

"Walton...damn, you really do know everything."

"How does this help me find Fowler?" I asked.

"So, the company. Translantic. I figured it would be an abandoned building or something. But I got curious, you know? I don't do many corporate jobs. So I looked them up. And it turns out, they're right here in New Lyons." My screen suddenly chimed. "And I just sent the address and other information to you." He gave me a smile that almost begged me to ask him how he'd gotten my number. I didn't bother. "So, we're good, right?"

I looked at Hernandez. She shrugged.

"Yeah, Manny," I said. "We're good."

Outside, Hernandez and I exchanged a long, silent look while we waited for the car. "Too easy," Hernandez said.

"Way too fucking easy," I agreed.

"So, what now?"

"I guess we go pay the people at Translantic a visit. Maybe we'll get lucky." Luck hadn't seemed to have been on my side for most of this investigation. But without any other leads to fall back on, it was my best bet.

Chapter 15

The docks of New Lyons were a strange affair. The rising waters had changed the character of the bottom as the oceans reclaimed land that had, at one point, been covered with a bustling, industrious city. You could still see remnants of that city, if you looked out over what passed for New Lyons' harbor—the tops of decaying buildings thrusting like rocks from the waters, decorated with antennae and satellite dishes. Hundreds, maybe thousands, of ruins lurked out there, some making their presence known, others hiding just beneath the waves.

There were clear avenues, of course. Places where streets had once stretched, providing channels for the harbor pilots to guide the container ships through the maze, sometimes with just feet between the hulls and the steel-and-glass reefs waiting to rip out their sides or bottoms. It made the approach of the ships into a twisting and ponderous dance that could be beautiful to watch. The harbor was close enough to Floattown that I sometimes did exactly that, perched atop the roof of my building with a glass of whiskey and a pair of binoculars. It was better entertainment than most of the offerings on the screens.

The land-side harbor offices were much more mundane. Most people never see the business end of ports, which is probably for the best, since there isn't much to recommend them. A chain-link fence topped with three strands of sagging barbed wire ran for miles, slicing off a neat section of New Lyons. Numerous roads ran through that fence, each with its own security checkpoint.

The physical security was laughable in a way. The only real purpose of the fence was to mark a boundary. As with most things, the real security came from the cameras, sensors, and scanners scattered about the harbor.

A criminal might get in, and even out again, but they knew that the odds of making a true escape with all the watching eyes were razor slim. It boiled down to the fact that law enforcement and city officials were way more worried about cargo coming off the ships than they were about anyone or anything getting into the harbor from the city side.

Getting away with criminal activity in person was a real challenge in the age of zero privacy. Which made the killer I was after—and Silas, too, for that matter—all the more frustrating. Impressive in their own way, but definitely frustrating.

The cruiser pulled up to one of the checkpoints and Hernandez spoke a few quick words to the security guard—human, rather than synthetic, since there was a chance, albeit a small one, that a security guard might be required to cause harm to another person. She flashed her badge, and he started giving directions to Translantic's offices. The gate went up and we got moving again.

"This doesn't feel right, Campbell," Hernandez said as she took manual control of the car to follow the guard's directions through the winding roads and prefabbed buildings.

I nodded. "If Walton Biogenics is behind this, they shouldn't have gone to Manny. And if they did, they damn well should have covered their tracks better. I don't care how good Manny is—the people at Walton are almost sure to be better."

She nodded, but didn't say anything as she continued to drive through the harbor. We had worked together a few times before, and we had the kind of relationship that didn't require either of us to be talking. We could sit comfortably enough in silence. But something was different this time. There was a quality to her silence that was almost foreboding. I wondered at that, and then it hit me. Shit.

"What's going on, Jason?" she asked. "When Manny said he found a corporate trail, you knew right where it led, right back to Walton Biogenics. But all Walton makes these days is synthetics." She paused as she threaded the cruiser between two massive container trucks. "What have you gotten us into?"

I was silent for a moment, pondering my response. I wanted to believe that Melinda Hernandez, the tough, caring detective who had been one of my only real friends on the force, would share my views on synthetics; I wanted to believe that she would be as horrified as I was at the atrocities inflicted by the killer I hunted. I wanted to believe it...but I wasn't sure I did.

Coming clean, telling her about Silas, the murders, the conspiracies, all of it...telling her that I believed Walton Biogenics was suppressing evidence proving synthetics were, in fact, human... I could gain an ally. Or, and perhaps more likely, Hernandez could turn me in to the brass. If she did that, at best, I'd get suspended. At worst, I'd get fired, and everything I'd worked toward for the past decade would be taken from me. In either case, I'd lose the auspices and powers of the New Lyons Police Department to help me carry forward with the investigation—though, at this point, I knew that whatever happened, I *would* keep investigating.

She pulled to a stop before a metal building that looked like a portable construction office. There was no logo or sign advertising the owner of the structure—the only indication we were at the right place was the number stenciled by the door: 227. Even that looked temporary, the edges of the digits already beginning to curl away from the steel in the heat and humidity.

I was stalling. Hernandez put the cruiser in park and waited expectantly. The expression on her face said she was ready to wait a long, long time.

I knew that I had to tell her, but something told me that just going over the facts of the case wouldn't be enough. I needed to give her more. I needed to tell her the truth, not just about the case, but about me. About Annabelle. I had never spoken those words out loud, never told anyone the truth about the series of events that had defined not just my views on synthetics, but me, and led me down the path to becoming a soldier and, ultimately, a cop. But I knew that, if I wanted Hernandez's continued help, she needed to know.

I had to tell her. Everything.

Chapter 16

There was no easy way to go about it, no easy way to tell the story. After all, how did one tell a law enforcement officer—even if that officer was a friend—that they were a convicted killer? I certainly didn't want to just blurt that out, and lose Hernandez before I even started.

"What's the problem, Campbell?" she said.

"Just trying to decide where to begin," I replied with a shrug.

"At the beginning," she said at once. "And then go on to the middle. And so on."

I felt a slight smile stretch my lips. "The beginning was a long time ago, Detective. A very long time."

"Well, we're not going one step more until I know what the hell is going on. And I'm sure whatever lead we might find in that office is going to get more and more nervous the longer you wait. Might do something stupid." She gave me a sour grin. "So you better get on with it."

I snorted at that. It was a classic cop tactic, adding a little time pressure to the interrogation. I couldn't blame Hernandez—she probably didn't even realize she'd done it. Instead, I said, "When did you meet your first synthetic?"

"Shit, Campbell. I don't know. We're about the same age. They started getting more available...what, twenty years ago? Thirty, maybe? Seems like by the time I got out of high school, they were everywhere, doing all the manual labor." A brief frown of distaste twisted her features. "And taking over all the sex-worker jobs. Sometime around then, I guess. When I was still in school, but I can't remember the specifics."

"Not many people can," I said. "Oh, almost everyone who actually *owns* a synthetic remembers when they got it. Assholes like Fortier can go into graphic details around the acquisition process. For them, it's like how getting your first car used to be, back before the ride share programs and self-driving vehicles..." I paused, closing my eyes for a moment, thinking back. It wasn't difficult. The memories were always there, just beneath the surface. "As for me, I met my first synthetic when I was twelve years old."

I ignored the pain that stabbed through me as I said the words aloud and fought down the memories that seemed to dance kaleidoscope-like behind my eyes. "I didn't know she was a synthetic at the time. She was just a girl, a pretty girl in a pretty dress who crossed paths with me when I was wandering around the neighborhood." I could see her in my mind's eye, golden locks and dimples and an air of innocence and wonder. She had been—at least to my puberty-clouded eyes—the most beautiful creature I'd ever seen.

"You don't see many synthetics that young," Hernandez said.

"No," I agreed. "You don't. Though I didn't learn that she was a synthetic until we were both seventeen."

"Wait. What?" I saw the barrage of questions that suddenly boiled up in Hernandez's eyes, but I raised one placating hand to forestall them.

"Her owners." I paused. Swallowed. Fought down the flashes of blood and rage and the sudden feel of flesh yielding before the crushing strength of my hands. Fought to keep the pain and anger from my voice. "Her owners," I said again, "masqueraded her as their daughter, rather than as a synthetic. As far as I've been able to learn, they kept the fact that she was anything other than their...their daughter...from the entire town."

"But...that's illegal. And is it even possible? I thought synthetics were programmed so they couldn't try to pass for human."

A bitter smile twisted my lips. "Hernandez, if being illegal stopped people from doing things, we'd be out of a job. As for being possible, what does passing for human mean? I never asked her if she was a synthetic. I'm sure nobody else did. She was a little girl—why would they? She certainly never volunteered the information. Probably had been commanded not to. Everyone who saw her just assumed she was a person, like you or me."

I sighed. "And she became my friend, Melinda. You may have noticed, I don't have very many of those. It was a little better when I was a kid, but not much. We lived away from town, the kind of place where there were only a dozen houses within a mile or two, far enough outside the New Lyons sprawl that we didn't have access to public transportation to get to places. So friends were few and far between and normally only around during school or the infrequent birthday party or get-together. But her family"—my lips twisted on the word—"moved in down the street. So, we inevitably found each other, the way kids always seem to. Started to hang out. Grew close. Grew inseparable. She made me feel good, Mel. Happy. Important. She was always glad to see me, and I was always glad to see her. Her name was Annabelle."

I lapsed into silence again, mind drifting back across those early years, before everything had gone so horrifically wrong and our biggest concerns were homework and finding new ways to escape from under our parents' thumbs. Or so I had thought.

"Bastards," Hernandez spat.

I arched an eyebrow at her.

"The synthetic's owners," she said in response. "To mess with people's heads that way."

I shook my head. Hernandez was right, and more than right, as she didn't yet know the half of it. And at the same time, she was completely missing the point. "They were that. And worse. But they were good at what they did. They kept their secret. For years."

"But why?" she asked. "What was the point?"

It was something I had considered over the years. I had long since come to my own conclusions, my own answer to the question. "Control. And to feel superior. To feel smarter than everyone around them. To get one over on all their neighbors." I felt an unconscious snarl starting to curl my lips, and I forced them into a tight line. "They liked to be in control."

Hernandez tilted her head, clearly sensing there was more to the story. But she waited. Not patiently. No cop was great at waiting patiently. But she waited nonetheless.

"Things changed a couple of years later. Annabelle"—it still hurt to say her name out loud—"showed up at my door. Asked me to go for a walk. Ordered me, really," I said with a sad smile. "I could tell something was wrong. I could tell she was in pain. Physical pain. Emotional pain. But I was too much the dumb scared teen to do anything about it. So I walked with her. For hours. Not saying anything. Not daring to touch her. Sensing somehow that she needed me there, but that human"—I spat the word—"contact was the last thing she wanted. I didn't get it. Not then. Though it became painfully obvious later."

"They abused her?" Hernandez asked, her voice subdued.

"They *raped* her, Melinda. I mean, she was just a synthetic, right?" I heard the venom in my words and tried to choke it off, but couldn't. "It started almost as soon as she turned fourteen. A fourteen-year-old girl, but hey, just a synthetic. In the eyes of the law, she couldn't be abused.

Couldn't be raped. But she had feelings, Mel, emotions. I could see the fear. The betrayal. The hopelessness, even if I was too dumb to say anything."

We were silent for a long moment before I drew a deep breath and let it out in a sigh. "We started dating not too long after that. Fell into it, really. It just seemed the next, natural step, the inevitable progression of our friendship. I should have realized something was wrong, especially when I met her 'parents' with their snide smiles and mocking glances. With the long, measuring looks they threw my way, like they were trying to decide if I was the butt of the joke or in on it. I should have suspected something, but I was just a kid, Hernandez."

I smiled, the first genuine smile in what felt like a long time as my mind wandered back over those years. "We had some good times, those first couple of years. All the normal teenagers-in-love bullshit that seems so ridiculous now, but at the time was the most important thing in my life. There were signs of what she was going through at home, the abuse, the kind of thing that we've been trained to recognize, but I couldn't see them. Shit. Maybe I didn't *want* to see them. Didn't want to confront that reality."

My smile faded. "And then everything changed." I shifted in my seat, easing the pressure where my pistol dug into my side, as if reminding me of the lethal potential we all carried within us. "When I was seventeen, I killed Annabelle's parents."

Chapter 17

"What?" Hernandez sat bolt upright in her seat, her eyes, which had been scanning the parking lot, locking on mine. I stared back at her, my face calm, despite the roiling of my stomach.

"I killed them," I repeated, forcing my voice to normalcy.

She kept her stare for a long moment, then drew a steadying breath. "If you murdered them, you couldn't be a cop. Not now. Not ever. Shit. We're talking twenty, twenty-five years ago. You wouldn't be out, walking around. Your ass would still be in jail. So, it must have been something else." Her expression had taken on a sharper edge, a little anger in it now, a little doubt. As if she was wondering if I was the same person she'd worked with, trained with, been friends with for the past few years. "What the hell happened, *hermano*?"

"I went to pick her up at her house," I replied. "Just like any other day. But when I got to the door, I heard a scream. I was inside before I knew what I was doing, moving up the stairs. There was the sound of an impact, something striking flesh, another muffled scream. It was coming from the door to Annabelle's parents' room. I didn't think. Didn't make a conscious decision. Maybe all the signs I'd been seeing for years added up all at once. Maybe, on some level, I knew what I was going to find. What I was going to have to do. Whatever the reason, I kicked the door open."

I closed my eyes and could see it, as clearly as if it had happened only the day before and not twenty-something years ago. Most of the room was a standard master suite. A large bed, dressers, doors leading to what I assumed were either closets or bathrooms. No carpet here, just a tile floor in a cold, institutional white. Next to the bed stood a piece of furniture for which, at the time, I had no name. Wooden braces formed an A-shaped frame, maybe six feet tall at its peak, four or five feet wide on the long sides, and three feet wide along the shorter edges. Boards crossed the front side of the frame, forming an X.

Annabelle hung there, arms above her head, legs spread-eagle, bound to the boards at wrist and ankle. She wore not a stitch of clothing, but there was nothing alluring about her nudity. Her pale, revealed skin only served to call attention to the thin red welts raised on her stomach and thighs, and the bright crimson trickles of blood that seeped from long, narrow cuts on the slopes of her breasts. A ring gag had been forced into her mouth, held in place by leather straps. Her eyes widened as I stepped into the room, and I could see the fear in them, the pain, the regret...and above all, the shame.

I described the scene to Hernandez, as coldly as I could manage, categorizing it like I would any other crime scene, forcing the words out, one by one, and doing my best to choke back the rage that boiled alongside the memories.

"She wasn't alone," Hernandez said.

It wasn't a question, but I nodded anyway. "She was not. I didn't realize it at first. All I could see was the girl I loved, hanging there, naked and afraid. Then I heard the laughter." My fists tightened until my knuckles turned white, and it took a concerted effort to not slide my hand down to my sidearm, to feel the reassuring weight of its cold lethality.

"Shit, Campbell."

"Yeah. Her 'parents' were there. Both of them."

I ground my teeth and stopped again, in part because the memories were painful enough already, and about to get worse. But only in part. Killing Annabelle's owners was a secret I had carried for a long time, through both my military and law enforcement careers. I had no doubt that my superiors in the army and on the force had learned some of the details—every good commanding officer, whether they wore green or blue, found out everything they could about the men and women under their command, through every channel possible. My records might have been sealed, but in the digital age, nothing was ever truly forgotten.

Still, I had managed to avoid any direct conversations around the details of the events that took place upon that day so long ago. And I had never, not even to my parents, divulged the one fact that would have irrevocably altered the course of my life. I killed Annabelle's owners, yes. But as far as the courts knew, it was an act committed before I knew the truth about Annabelle, before I knew that she was a synthetic.

I was on her "father" before his smug laughter had finished sounding, true, but at first all I'd done was deliver a good hard right to his face. And he had only laughed harder. His words, diamond hard and with as much soul, were burned into my brain. I could recall them verbatim, even now. "You little shit," he had said around his guffaws. "She's a toy. A fucking mule. A synthetic. She's our goddamned *property*. And you're what? In love with her? Going to save her? Might as well be in love with a toaster, you insufferable little puke. Get the hell out, before we call the cops."

I hadn't, of course. I couldn't. When I had done what I had done, I had known the truth. And I'd been holding tight to that truth ever since. It was, most likely, the only reason that I was not locked up in some corporate-run factory prison. But did I risk telling Hernandez the truth? Did I burden her with the knowledge that I was, as far as the law was concerned, very likely a murderer? Oh, the case was long since closed, and couldn't be reopened, whatever facts might come to light. I was in no legal danger from anyone knowing the truth. But if I told Hernandez, then it would become her secret to bear—or not—as well. I couldn't do that to her, couldn't put that burden upon her. Couldn't take that risk. So I stuck to the "official" version of events.

"I lost it," I said. "Seeing the man who was supposed to be her father standing there like that, laughing at me as he abused the girl I loved. I attacked him. I must have surprised him—I guess he was used to blind obedience. This was long before I'd had any actual training, but I was a big, athletic kid. I knocked him down with a couple of quick punches, powered more by rage and youth rather than any real skill. And then I kicked him. A single kick, just to shut him the hell up, to stop that cutting, mocking laughter. It caught him just beneath the chin." I could still feel the crackle of cartilage crushing under the force of the blow, the shock of pain and the savage satisfaction it brought. "It was an accident. At least, I don't think I meant to kill him. But the kick crushed his windpipe and, I learned later, the force ruptured his carotid. He was dead within seconds. We were all too shocked, too stunned, to do anything but watch him die." That much, at least, was true.

"And the 'mother'?" Hernandez asked, her voice neutral. I almost winced at her tone. I'd heard it before. I'd *used* it before. It was the tone most cops got when a suspect was confessing to a particularly heinous crime and you had to let them finish before leveling the charges. It was a sterile, neutral, institutional kind of tone, bereft of any emotion. It wasn't the kind of tone you ever wanted to hear from a friend.

There was no going back now. "She lost it. Screamed an animal scream. I thought she was going to attack me. But she didn't. Instead, she went for Annabelle."

The memory was there, waiting, when I closed my eyes.

Annabelle's mother stood before her, screaming incoherently, face reddened from the effort. In one hand she held a long, narrow-bladed knife. Part of my mind recognized it as a filleting knife, used to scale fish or cut very thin slices of meat. The needlelike tip had doubtless been the instrument to carve the fine lines of blood into the slopes of Annabelle's breasts, and was probably responsible for many of the scars that crisscrossed her body.

I should have feared that knife. I should have feared the woman wielding it. But all I felt was an ice-cold rage. I took one step toward her, and her eyes widened. Her screaming shut off midcry, and a calculating look replaced the terror in her eyes. A cruel smile twisted her lips, and she spun without warning.

I had just enough time to raise a hand in denial as the knife blade plunged between Annabelle's breasts. A violent shudder coursed through her, rattling the frame from which she hung. Her eyes met mine a final time, and I watched, helpless, as the light slowly faded from them.

Annabelle's mother and I stared at each other, bookended by the corpses of the people we loved. There was no more screaming, now, no shouts of defiance or anger or loss. One of us was going to die. I saw it in her eyes, and had no doubt she could see it in mine. Her fingers were still curled around the knife, and she pulled, trying to yank the blade from Annabelle's corpse.

The body heaved, bucked, but the blade did not move.

Synthetics were not supposed to be able to defy their owners. Whether or not Annabelle had managed it in life, she found defiance in death. She would not let go of the blade. That almost certainly saved my life. I stepped forward again, now just one long stride from Annabelle's mother. My hands flexed, fingers curling.

I shook the images from my mind. "The bitch killed her," I said. "Out of spite. Drove a knife right into Annabelle's heart. And then she came for me. Maybe I didn't mean to kill Annabelle's 'father.' Maybe. To this day, I'm still not certain about that. But I damn sure meant to kill her bitch of a 'mother.' It was a brutal, dirty fight. She had that stupid little riding crop, and she knew how to use it." I drew one finger along the corner of my eye, where a small white scar ran. "She almost took my eye. But it was more a toy than a weapon, something designed to hurt, but not injure, not kill, meant for the pain-is-pleasure crowd. I got my hands around her throat, and no matter the punishment she laid upon me, I didn't let go. It was easy. So damn easy. I could still see Annabelle, hanging there, still and lifeless with the hilt of a knife sticking from her chest. I didn't let go for a long, long time. When I finally did, I was alone in a room of corpses."

Chapter 18

"*Jesu Christo*, Campbell," Hernandez breathed.

"Yeah," I grunted. "You can imagine what happened next. I called the cops. I was taken into custody. Fortunately for me, my parents had a good lawyer."

"Two dead bodies. You don't just walk away from that, *hermano*, not with a record clean enough to land a job as a cop a couple of decades later."

"No," I admitted. "But everyone in the whole damn town felt betrayed by Annabelle's owners. Felt like they'd been played the fool by having the sweet little girl turn out to be a synthetic." My face twisted hard at that. In some ways, I owed those raping bastards for helping me realize the truth, though I would have gladly lived on in ignorance if it meant Annabelle would still be alive. "Still, they couldn't ignore the corpses. No one cried murder, not when the facts came to light, but they couldn't just call it self-defense, either. The DA wanted to file for manslaughter."

"And?" she asked.

"And I cut a deal. Or my lawyer did, anyway. This was a long time ago, Hernandez. We were still embroiled in a dozen different conflicts in every desert and hellhole on the map. The army was hungry for bodies, and I didn't want to serve any time. So, my lawyer got the DA to agree to an enlistment in place of jail. A five-year stint, at a time when I was almost guaranteed to see combat, and a clean record when I got out. Or be tried as an adult, spend ten years in jail, and have a felony conviction on my record forever after." I snorted, shrugged. "It seemed like an easy decision at the time."

"*Jesu Christo*," she said again.

"Yeah, well. That's the background—my background—but that ain't it, Hernandez. The murders I've been chasing? The victims? All female. All synthetics. All horribly mutilated." I gave her all the details. I told her about Silas and his warnings, about all the leads and dead ends that I'd chased for the past—shit, had it only been two days? I told her the real reasons behind the laws surrounding the disposal of synthetics and the ban on genetic testing. All of it. The only bit I left out was Tia Morita and the blood tests she'd run—there was no sense in implicating the coroner's assistant in any of it.

"Synthetics are people, Hernandez," I said at the end. "As much people as you and I, no matter how they were created. People who think and feel and desire. And we treat them like slaves—worse than slaves. All of us, every fucking society on the face of the planet. We claim to be advanced, but we do things to our own that would make our ancestors blush, all under the pretense that they aren't—can't be—human. It's bullshit."

Hernandez opened her mouth as if to speak, but I kept talking, steamrolling right over her. "You probably think I'm crazy, but I've seen it, Melinda. I've *seen* it, for myself. Not whatever irrefutable proof that Silas claims is being suppressed by Walton Biogenics. We don't even need that, not if we're being honest with ourselves. Annabelle may have helped me open my eyes, but even without what happened to me, to her, it's there. The proof is all around us. It's like I've been asleep for twenty years, and these last few days have finally woken me the hell up. All you have to do is talk to a synthetic—not give them orders, but actually *talk* to them. Oh, sure, all you're likely to get is whatever response they've been trained—trained, conditioned, not programmed—to say, but look at them while they do it. Really *look*. You can see the thoughts behind the facade—the fear, and yes, the hate. But can you blame them?"

I was babbling and I knew it. With an effort, I forced myself to stop talking. It took an even greater effort to turn and look Hernandez in the eye. Her expression was...troubled.

"For fuck's sake, Campbell," she said with a long sigh. Her hands were wrapped tight around the steering wheel, as if to prevent them from shaking. "You can't just unload that on me."

I shrugged, embarrassed. "Well...you did ask."

"Fuck. This is going to kill our careers, you know. Pensions right out the window. We're going to have to live on stipends for the rest of our days." The words came out barely above a whisper, and there was some deep emotion that I couldn't quite make out lingering beneath that tone. But she had said "we."

"You believe me?" I asked, struggling to keep the incredulity out of my voice.

"Yes. No. Shit. I don't know," she growled. "All that shit about sealed records that Fortier was blathering on about makes sense, at least." I saw the anger in the set of her jaw, in the white-knuckled tightening of her fingers on the steering wheel. Hernandez was pissed...but I didn't think she was pissed at me. Or at least, not only at me.

"You don't have to be a part of this, Hernandez," I said. "Just drop me off and head back to the precinct. Just...don't tell the brass what I'm doing." I didn't have the right to ask that of her. By the book, she should report me. I asked anyway.

"Fuck you, Campbell. You think I'm just going to leave you here when you think your life is in danger? Do you understand just how much shit you're in? If what you say is true...Christ." I could almost see the chain of thoughts going through her head, just as they had for me in my conversation with Silas. If this came out, society had three choices: acknowledge that it was built on absolute oppression and maintain the status quo; stick its collective head in the sand and pretend nothing happened; or outright revolution. And since "society" wasn't really a singular thing, but rather a bunch of people who would make their own—and almost certainly contradictory—decisions, there was zero chance of anything happening without violence. Probably widespread and likely indiscriminate.

But the alternative was to allow an entire population of people to be completely and totally subjugated, to continue to be stripped of every right that we still dared to call inalienable. I couldn't let that stand—not anymore—regardless of the consequences. And from the struggle on Hernandez's face, neither could she.

"I have a synth nanny, you know?" she said, in an apparent non sequitur. "She takes care of Arlene." Arlene was Hernandez's daughter. She never said much about her family. All I knew was that she was a single mother and her daughter was somewhere between walking and high school. "It took me years to save up, to afford her. She must have been beautiful once, but she's older now. Older than me. I'm not sure what she did before. But there's a look in her eyes sometimes. I told myself I was imagining things. She looks at my daughter with such love. But sometimes, sometimes there's something else there." She paused, and a flash of uncertainty passed across her face. "I don't know, Campbell. In anything—anyone—else..." She stopped again, brow furrowing, obviously reaching for the right word. "I'd call it hate. Deep, deep hate." She looked at me, and I could see the tears forming in the corner of her eyes. "Not just of me. But of Arlene, too. What kind of life must she have lived, to look at a child with that kind of hate?"

"You know what kind of life, Hernandez," I said gently. "We all know. And we all close our eyes and turn our heads away and console ourselves with the thought that it's OK, because they aren't human. Just things." I shook my head, disgusted, not with Hernandez, but with myself. With all the years that I had spent silently ignoring a truth that was plain to see, if one only bothered to look at it.

It was Hernandez's turn to be quiet for a long moment. Then, as if she had made a decision, she checked her weapon with one hand and opened the car door with the other. "Let's go," she said.

I couldn't help but smile as I got out of the car. Whatever else happened, I wasn't alone.

Chapter 19

The Translantic offices left a lot to be desired.

The building, if it could be called that, was little more than a metal trailer. The door had a flimsy screen feel to it, and I doubted it would have kept out a determined raccoon, much less someone with criminal intent. The interior wasn't much better. The room within was tiny—though even at tiny it still took up half of the "office." A door off to the right marked Private must have led to the rest of the space.

There was a single desk, wedged in to one end of the narrow rectangular space with barely enough room between the edge of the desk and the unadorned wall to allow a person to slip through. There were no chairs in front of that desk, nothing to show that visitors were common or even welcome.

A screen sat atop the desk, and behind it sat a rather unprepossessing man. Average height, average build, unremarkable limp brown hair. Even his face held that nondescript everyman quality. He was, in every way, forgettable. If this was my killer, he could disappear into any crowd, anywhere and I'd likely never find him again. I didn't think he was my killer, though. Something about the way he started as we entered the office didn't exactly scream "hardened criminal" or even "corporate hatchet man." More like timid desk jockey.

"Can I help you?" he asked. "This isn't really a public office, you know."

We flashed our badges. The shields earned us a nervous twitch. "Are these the offices of Translantic Shipping?" I asked.

"Yes," he replied cautiously.

"And are you the only employee?" Hernandez asked.

The man shrugged. "I'm the only employee here. At this location, I mean. What's this all about?"

I ignored his question, and kept asking my own. "What is it you do here, Mr...."

"Eggleston. Adam Eggleston. I manage logistics."

"What kind of logistics?"

"Arrival and departure of various cargoes," he said, a note of impatience beginning to creep into his voice. "Look, if you tell me what you want, maybe I can help."

Hernandez held up her phone. On it was a zoomed and enhanced image of the man who had entered Manny's shop—the man we knew only as Jeremy Fowler. "Can you identify this man?"

The man glanced at the phone, and the color slowly drained from his face. He swallowed once then cleared his throat. "I'm afraid not," he said, his voice suddenly too loud in the small room. "Never seen him before in my life."

As he spoke, his hand dipped searchingly into his desk. It wasn't the sudden jerk of someone going for a weapon, though my hand instinctively moved to the butt of my service weapon. Hernandez did the same, taking a half step away from me and turning so that she was facing the clerk at more of an angle. Presenting a smaller target.

Eggleston was still talking, almost tripping over his words. "Look, I've been more than cooperative here, but I've got a lot of work to do. I haven't seen whoever that is, OK? I really need to get back to my job. And I've got a meeting in a few minutes. It really would be best if you left now."

While he talked, his hands continued to work, pulling a scrap of paper from somewhere in his desk. He scrawled something on it, keeping his body upright, in a weird, awkward position. Keeping, I realized, his hands out of frame of whatever security camera must be watching him. He shoved one hand across the desk, palm down, covering whatever note he had scrawled.

I took the hint. "Of course, Mr. Eggleston. We'd hate to keep you from your work." I dug around in my jacket pocket and fished out another card, offering it to him. "My information, in case you think of anything that might be useful."

He nodded, an exaggerated expression of relief plastered across his face. For my benefit, or the watching electronic eyes? As I handed him the card, I felt him slide the slip of paper into my hand in return. "Of course, Officer. Anything I can do to help."

I nodded again, curtly. Hernandez did the same, and we turned and went back out the door. Once in the relative safety of the cruiser, Hernandez raised an eyebrow at me. "Well? What does it say?"

I turned the note over in my hand. The ink had smeared a bit, testament to the sweaty palms of the clerk, but it was still legible. It read *Container C-347A 22:00. Come alone.* I tilted my hand to show the message to Hernandez.

She looked at it and snorted, somewhere between amusement and disgust. "A clandestine meeting," she grunted. "And you're supposed to go it alone. Did these people learn to do this by watching old spy movies?"

"Corporate criminals," I reminded her. "Competent in their own endeavors, I'm sure. But this stinks of a setup. Which makes sense. Manny's place stunk from the start."

"What's our next move?"

I was grateful that she was still saying "our." I shrugged. "I guess we head back to the precinct, see if anything else has come in. And then I get ready to walk into a trap."

Chapter 20

The precinct was a bust. My searches were still running, and Hernandez had already exhausted her sources. Neither of us were particularly hungry, but we grabbed some dinner anyway, away from the precinct.

As we ate our burgers, Hernandez asked, "How are we going to do this?"

I shrugged. "We go back to the docks. I go to the container alone, with you close enough to come to the rescue if things go south."

She stared at me in incredulity. "Are you out of your fucking mind? You think I'm going to let you walk in blind, while I what...wait in the car?"

"We don't have a lot of choice, Hernandez," I said with a sigh. "Look, you think it's a trap. I think it's a trap. But it's the only lead we've got. If I don't go, or if we go in loaded for bear with half the cops in New Lyons, we aren't going to find anything. There's a chance, however slim, that this is a legit meet, and I can't ignore that. So we have to play along. Which means I go in alone."

"And get your dumb ass killed," she snapped.

"Maybe. But if it is a death trap and you go in with me, it's just as likely that we both get killed. And the investigation dies with us. Look, you know I'm former military, right? I've been in ambush situations before. I know what to look for. Even if it's a trap, I've got a good chance of spotting it and bugging the fuck out or hunkering down before things go completely sideways. And if they do go sideways, you can be damn sure that I'm going to be in need of some backup. That's where you come in. The only 'wait in the car' you'll do is if everything is hunky dory and the meet is legit. In which case," I said with finality, "coming in with me would be pointless anyway."

She bit down angrily on a fry, chewing it with a savage intensity. "I still think you're going to get your ass killed," she mumbled around the food. "But fine. Whatever, *pendejo*. It's your ass."

* * * *

The stacked containers formed mountains with narrow passes stretching between them like alleyways. The smell of the ocean competed with the more acrid tangs of marine fuel, exhaust, and rusting steel, clinging to containers with the heaviness of a wet fog in the still night air. Far overhead, automated cranes moved silently on impressive track systems, a silence that shattered each time a cable and electromagnet plunged earthward from them, clamping onto one of the metal boxes with a sound like impending apocalypse. Since most of the loading and off-loading of the containers was handled by a variety of unmanned systems, lights were few and far between, leaving long pools of inky shadows throughout most of the container storage area.

"Why meet here?" I muttered to myself, partly because the question was on my mind, and partly to hear a human voice among the darkness and machinery. "Remote enough to kill someone—not a lot of watchful eyes." A crane dropped its magnet onto a nearby container, the noise sudden and loud enough that my hand went instinctively to my sidearm. "And loud enough to cover any screams or cries for help." The metal box, filled with who knew what, lifted silently into the night sky. I followed its progress, fascinated by the smooth, rapid ascent.

Watching it saved my life.

Perched atop one of the mountains of crates, I caught the briefest glint of reflected light, winking at me like a watching eye. I reacted on instinct, and felt foolish even as I did, diving into a long, low roll that sent me crashing up against the edge of one of the containers. I felt less foolish as I saw the puff of pulverized concrete and heard the impact of something very small and moving fast strike the ground near where I had been standing.

I'd seen no muzzle flash and heard no report, but someone had just tried to kill me. My roll had taken me behind a wall of containers, outside the line of sight of the gunman—at least, I hoped it was just one gunman. I kept my eyes up, scanning the uneven skyline of shipping containers, looking for any sign of a lurking sniper. The darkness made it nearly impossible. I was a sitting duck, a target, as long as I remained at ground level. "Shit."

My forty-five was in my hand, though I didn't remember pulling it. I levered myself to my feet, using the container against which my back rested as support. Then I took off in a quick run, keeping the wall to my left, eyes searching the container tops, but also looking for a ladder or scaffolding or something that would facilitate gaining some high ground. I tried to keep my breathing steady, even as I ran. The container yard offered my assailant—or assailants, I still didn't know which—lots of high perches from which to take potshots at me, but it was still a long way from the ideal setup for a sniper. The deep, narrow alleyways between the walls of crates afforded little in the way of sight lines, and gave me plenty of opportunities to cut around a corner and break from view. So, if this was a setup, which had seemed painfully obvious even before the bullets started flying, why here?

Another electromagnet thrummed and crashed into a nearby tower, and I cursed under my breath. Yeah, that was a pretty good reason. I crouched low next to a sheltering wall, eyes still scanning, as I dug my screen from my pocket. I shrouded the display as much as possible, not wanting its backlit glass to light up my face and send a bright red flare to my would-be killers, but I had to know. Hernandez was out there, waiting for me, the cavalry ready to come crashing in to save my ass. "Son of a bitch," I cursed as I stared at the screen. Two words that were, most of the time, only a minor annoyance greeted my quick glance: No Signal. Between the towers of rusting metal and the superpowered magnets dangling from a network of steel tracks and cables, I might as well have been in the world's most elaborate Faraday cage. If Hernandez came in blind, she'd be walking into the same death trap that I currently found myself enjoying.

OK. Maybe not trained snipers, not with the shitty sight lines. But not stupid, either. Smart enough to isolate me, cut me off from backup. What to do?

I had to assume this was the work of Walton Biogenics. "Come on, Campbell," I whispered to myself. *If you were a megarich multinational corporation hell bent on keeping your dirty laundry from becoming public,* I thought, *and a too-curious cop kept sticking his nose in, how would you take him out?*

Item one on the assassination list would, of course, be isolation. I certainly wasn't important enough to warrant making a political statement through a public execution, and it was a lot easier to make a getaway when no one else was around. Plus, cops had guns and training and the ability to call more people with guns and training, and if I was going to be assassinating someone, I'd want to be the one with all the firepower and backup. I glanced around the deserted docks and stuffed my useless screen back into my pocket. Isolation. Check. Which brought me to item two on the list: backup. Sure, the lone gunman had a certain sense of the romantic, but in the real world, numbers matter, and it's much easier to take someone out if you outnumbered them. Which meant that it was possible, even likely, that there was more than one bad guy making their way through the containers, and I had more to worry about than just the sniper. But how would I use that backup?

I almost laughed—a reaction driven more by fear and nerves than any sense of humor at my situation. I'd have my backup sitting in a car, waiting for a call from a place with no fucking service, apparently. But if I wasn't an idiot, how would I do it?

The deep and narrow alleys formed by the stacked containers made for a complicated shooting scenario for even a gifted sniper. On the other hand, they made perfect kill boxes for guys on the ground. Normally the beaters would drive the prey into the shooter's sights, but I had the distinct impression that the sniper's job wasn't so much to kill me as it was to contain me, no pun intended, keeping me in place until the shooters on the ground could find me and finish the job. The place was a maze, but I knew that if I stepped out from shelter offered by the containers and into the open, I wouldn't have to worry about Silas breaking into my place anymore.

And that left me with some serious problems. If I went high, like I'd originally intended, I'd open myself up to fire from the guy or guys with rifles. If I stayed low, assuming I was right, I'd eventually run into the guys on the ground. I could dig in, find a defensible position and fort up, hoping the bad guys either didn't find me, or that the twenty-five rounds of forty-five ACP ammunition I had on me would stand up to whatever firepower they were packing. No. Once the noisy shooting started, Hernandez would come crashing in, and she'd be an easy target for the sniper. Assuming, I thought with a sinking feeling, that the sniper hadn't taken the first shot at the cruiser parked a little ways away from the stacks. Shit. I needed to get out, and I needed to do it in a way that wouldn't give the guys with the long guns a clear shot at me or point them toward Hernandez.

"Guess I'm going to get wet," I muttered.

I stayed low and kept tight to the containers. I didn't head for the car that Hernandez had parked just outside the maze. Instead, I pushed east, moving toward the sound of crashing waves and the smell of salt water. There was too much space on the landward side of the container yard, too many clear sight lines that would guarantee me a bullet even if I managed to avoid the guys I knew had to be in here with me. I didn't know what the other side looked like—there had to be space between the containers and the actual docks, roads, and the like to facilitate transshipment, but it still seemed like a better chance than moving back toward the city.

My breathing was coming low and fast now, despite efforts to force it into a regular rhythm and, more importantly, to quiet it. I moved quickly, padding along the concrete somewhere between a walk and a run, scanning and listening, weapon at the ready, always hugging the steel containers. Between the waves and the machinery, I couldn't hear a damn thing. On the one hand, that meant the bad guys probably couldn't hear me...but it also increased the odds of blundering into them before any of us knew it by a not-insignificant amount.

I rounded a corner and, as if summoned by my musings, very nearly ran into a large man in black combat fatigues. I got only a general impression, a darker shape against the poorly lit night: over six feet tall, thick through the chest and shoulders, balaclava reducing his face to just a pair of cold blue eyes. Mostly, I registered the shotgun, a pistol-gripped combat variety dwarfed by his meaty hands, and the fact that he had two buddies right behind him.

As a cop, I should have demanded he stop right there, drop his weapon, and surrender like a good little criminal. But in that moment, I wasn't a cop. I wasn't even a soldier. I was just a guy, outnumbered and alone, and afraid that I wasn't going to make it home.

I reacted an instant faster than my would-be killers, and in that instant, I could have pulled the trigger. I might even have been able to put down the first guy...before his two friends blasted me into my component atoms over his tumbling corpse. Instead I surged forward, moving in a low crouch, making sure the behemoth's body stayed firmly in place between me and the other guns. I jammed my left arm under the gun, shearing the barrel of the shotgun up and away, pointing the weapon up toward the night sky. His finger must have been on the receiver, rather than the trigger, because the sudden motion didn't result in the deafening boom that I had been half expecting. I jammed the tang of the forty-five into the back of his thigh, using it as a hook and pulling toward me as I jammed my shoulder into his gut and shoved off with my legs.

He was big. Two twenty, maybe two thirty, and built like a linebacker, but the biggest guy in the world can be bowled over pretty easy when you combine surprise with the push-pull action of the takedown I executed. I could have used that move to drive him into the ground, but that would have left me open to less-than-friendly fire. Instead, I used the driving force of my legs and a shoving heave from my left arm to half push, half throw him at the two men moving in tight formation on his six.

My right shoulder dug into his gut as I hurled the man into his associates. They went down like bowling pins, and I had a sudden, almost giddy desire to yell, "Strike!" Instead, I put rubber to pavement and sprinted past, barely breaking my stride. I remembered to keep close to the containers, taking the shelter that I could from them. A gunshot—not the silenced rasp of the sniper rifle, but the throaty bellow of a shotgun—sounded behind me, and I winced as I heard the buckshot slam into the metal of one of the crates and ricochet like lead rain.

Had Hernandez heard that over the crash and clatter of the shipping containers and cranes? And if she had, what would she do? If she came tearing in, guns blazing... But, then again, if she didn't... Shit.

I ducked my head and ran faster, taking turns at random, but always moving steadily toward the siren song of the sea. At least three men on the ground, and one, somewhere, with a rifle. Four-to-one odds, at best, and that assumed no second team of hitters that I could barrel into at any moment. Angry shouts and cursing followed me, thinned, and then stopped altogether. I stopped with it, crouching once more in the shadows, panting as quietly as I could, ears straining.

I had lost them in the maze of containers, and was now engaged in a deadly game of hide-and-seek. The same electromagnetic trap that had rendered my screen useless probably had the same effect on anything short of military-grade radios, so they probably could only communicate with each other within shouting distance—and they weren't doing any more shouting. So, had they stayed together, or split up? If I were hunting me, I would have stayed together, keeping my firepower concentrated and making sure that if I found my prey, I could put it down for good. But then, I knew just how dangerous a hunt the bad guys had started. I wondered if they did. Sure, they knew I was a cop, but did they know about my military training? The action I'd seen in places that made Floattown look like the Ritz? My obsession with martial arts? They knew they had bigger guns and more men, and they knew that if I got away from them tonight, it was going to be a hell of a lot harder to lure me into a trap next time.

No, with what they knew, they wouldn't stay together. Splitting up would give them a much better chance of mission success. I felt a feral grin start to curl the corner of my lip as thoughts of escape were replaced by new and darker thoughts. If I could take these guys down, take even one of them in, then I would be able to get some answers. And if I could find a link from them back to Walton Biogenics…well, not even a company their size could simply shrug off the attempted murder of a police officer.

I slipped my pistol back into its holster and instead reached to my left hip. There was a small leather case there, and inside was an eight-inch cylinder of dense steel. I pulled the telescoping baton from its sheath and hit the quick-release button, transforming the slug of metal from eight inches to a two-foot-long carbon-steel rod. I gave it an experimental twirl as I pushed myself back to my feet. I was done being hunted. It was time to go to work.

I glided through the shadows, always conscious of the sight lines above me, always concerned about the potential for the shooter to have moved, sought a new position, found a better angle. But it was a worry at the back of my head, a risk I tried to mitigate by staying in cover, staying out of sight, but it was no longer my primary concern. One of my would-be killers stalked silently in front of me, shotgun held before him. It wasn't the linebacker—this one was smaller, more slender, almost wiry. Same black fatigues, and same pistol-grip combat shotgun, though. And, most importantly, this one didn't know that I was moving up behind him.

I closed the last ten feet in a sprint. It was impossible to do so silently—the soles of my shoes made an inevitable slapping noise against the concrete. But I didn't need to be silent, only fast. He heard me when I was five feet away and started to turn, bringing the shotgun to bear. But it was too late. I flicked the baton out in a quick, slashing strike. The rounded tip connected with the masked man's jaw with a bone-crunching *crack*, loud enough that I winced at the sound and sharp enough that I almost felt sympathy for the man as he crumpled, boneless, to the pavement.

I pulled my bracelets from the back of my belt and cuffed the man to the door of the closest container, then rifled through his pockets. No wallet, or ID, or anything useful, which wasn't terribly surprising. I pulled his mask from his face. He was an average-looking guy, mid- to late twenties, nondescript brown hair and with handsome, symmetrical features. Well, they had been. His jaw was already purpling and swelling, clearly broken.

I could snap a picture with my screen, but without the flash, it wouldn't be much good…and the flash would certainly alert the sniper, if not the ground crew, as to my location. "I'll be back for you, buddy," I whispered to the man as I did another quick search—this time for weapons. In addition to the shotgun, I found a 9mm automatic and a tactical folder. I stuck the knife in my pocket and grabbed the other weapons. They would only slow me down, so I stashed them in a narrow crack between two containers, a good fifteen feet from the downed killer.

"One down, two to go," I muttered to myself. Plus the shooter. If he was still out there. It occurred to me that he might not be. It hadn't exactly been a long time since that first shot was fired. No more than five or ten minutes had passed, even though I felt like this ordeal had been going on for hours. But if I couldn't reach the outside world from the trap they'd set, the shooter couldn't communicate with his minions, either. Which meant he couldn't spot, or direct, and could only rely on hearing gunshots to know the deed had been done. With the crash of the cranes, even those might be lost. How long would he wait before bugging out? Hell, for that matter, how long would Hernandez wait before coming in? We hadn't been real precise on our timelines, but I figured she would give me at least another ten or fifteen minutes before getting too antsy. If she hadn't heard that first shotgun blast.

I hadn't heard any other gunfire, though. Hernandez was almost as good with her hands and feet as I was, and more than capable of disabling someone without resorting to her sidearm. So she might be in among the crates already. The sniper had a silenced rifle, so there was a chance he had taken some shots that I wasn't aware of. Shots that might have found a home in Hernandez. That thought brought a chill deep in the pit of my stomach.

I moved as I pondered, low and slow, eyes and ears open. I caught the faint sound of footfalls approaching from behind and slid around the next corner I came to. I pressed my back against the steel and kept my hands before me, waiting, watching, listening. A few moments later, a second black-clothed killer padded into my field of view. He saw me at the same moment, turning toward me and bringing the shotgun up, the bore impossibly large as it swept in my direction. My baton was lighter, faster. I flicked it out, smashing a strike into the gunman's elbow, hitting with a meaty *thunk* even as I slid around the barrel and moved forward, getting inside its reach, pressing close against the guy and using my shoulder to keep the barrel from turning toward me.

He cried out in pain as the baton cracked the sensitive nerves of the elbow. His finger jerked spasmodically on the trigger and a second deafening boom shattered the night. Inwardly, I cursed, knowing the shot would bring the third gunman, the large one. It might also bring the sniper or Hernandez. But I didn't have time to dwell, as my baton was still in motion. The shot to the elbow might have been disabling—for that arm, anyway—but the bad guy was still on his feet and still a threat…and I didn't have much time before his friends arrived. I slashed the baton down, striking a knee, pivoting at the hips and back to ensure the strength of the strike despite the tight quarters. Another bone-breaking crack sounded. Before the man could fall, I was swinging again, this time driving the tip of the baton upward, catching the assassin just beneath the sternum and driving the steel into his midsection. The sound that came out of his mouth was something between a scream and a sigh as the air was driven from his lungs.

I let the baton continue up, snaking it between the gun and the man's torso, pushing it skyward until the butt of the baton had passed the man's head. I used the butt to hook behind my assailant's neck and then pivoted away, pulling down and toward my own body with the baton as I did so. The gunman spiraled down with astonishing speed—or he would have, if it weren't for the fact that I directed his fall full-on into the metal container. The sound of his head hitting the steel wall was reminiscent of a watermelon dropped on a concrete floor.

No time to search this one, cuff him, or even make sure he was alive. I hoped he was—I would already have too much explaining to do once all this came to light with the department. But I had to survive it first.

I made no effort at stealth. I sprinted away from the unconscious man and the target that the gunshot had made of him. Within the narrow alleyways of the container yard and the bouncing echoes all the metal and concrete guaranteed, the source of the shot would be hard to pinpoint. I figured I had only a few more seconds before the third man—the big man I had already bowled over once—appeared. It would have been the perfect opportunity to set a trap of my own, except for the pesky sniper, who definitely heard the shot and, from his no doubt elevated position, might well have seen the muzzle flash. I couldn't afford to hang out and risk coming into the long gunner's crosshairs.

That didn't mean I couldn't take advantage of the situation, though. I dug into my pockets. There wasn't much...some receipts, a pen, a couple of loose coins. It wasn't exactly breadcrumbs, but I judiciously dropped bits of flotsam as I ran, leaving a trail until I found what I was looking for. Amid the towering walls of containers, some stretching fifty, sixty feet or higher, I found a lone container, a stack of one, but still surrounded by its much taller fellows. It stood ten feet tall, an imposing cliff of steel. There was probably a ladder built into it somewhere, but I didn't bother trying to find it. Instead, I tucked my baton into my belt and sprinted toward the box. With an explosive leap, I was able to grasp the edge and pull myself up on top of the container, rolling over to my belly to watch back the way I had come.

It took longer than I'd expected, and that was a bad sign. A stupid adversary would have rushed to the sound of the gunfire and then followed my hastily laid trail at a sprint, angered by the injury to a friend and heedless of the danger. But the big man, it seemed, was far from stupid. He came cautiously, weapon advanced and at the ready, head sweeping back and forth in constant motion as he scanned for trouble. He was clearly a man expecting an ambush, and that made things a good bit harder for me.

I could have pulled my pistol and shot him where he stood. The soldier in me demanded it. But those same instincts that said shoot also screamed at me that this guy, the big, smart hunter, was the guy in the know, the guy that would be able to tell me how and where and why. Maybe even the mysterious Fowler himself. If I wanted answers, I needed him alive.

He padded forward, and I pushed myself up into a low crouch, moving back from the edge of the container as I did so, fading deeper into the shadows. With a few more steps, the gunman was in range. I took two quick strides and leapt, sailing out from the container. The man had enough time to turn, but I had caught him by surprise and he couldn't bring his gun to bear. I crashed into him and together we tumbled to the concrete. The shotgun was torn from his grip and I heard it slide away into the darkness.

We went down in a tangle of limbs, and even though I was prepared for it, the impact stunned me for a moment. Then we were both rolling apart, coming to our feet in almost mirror-image stances. I stood with my feet shoulder-width apart, left foot forward, balanced lightly on the balls of my feet. My arms were raised before me, left hand out front, right hand, my collapsible baton firmly clasped therein, slightly back, fist canted so that the tip of the baton was in line with my sternum. My would-be assailant had rolled to his feet as well, with an enviable smoothness that spoke of long training. He, too, stood in a fighting stance, crouched low, hands before him, fingers splayed. Our rolls had put us no more than six or eight feet apart. For a long moment, we just stared at each other, weighing, measuring.

He had a sidearm holstered at his hip. He hadn't tried to pull it. I hadn't gone for my gun, either. In the time it would take me to drop the baton and pull the pistol, he would already be on me. He was, at least, probably thinking the same thing behind the obscuring mask of the balaclava. He had size on me—not a lot, but enough. He was probably younger. His eyes crinkled around the corners, suggesting he was smiling at me. I couldn't see his lips, but I knew it would be an eager smile. Predatory. He flexed his fingers and I saw his legs start to bunch beneath him, readying for the forward surge.

I knew I was in trouble.

Chapter 21

"Right there!"

The shout, firm and authoritative, stopped both of us in our tracks. I recognized Hernandez's voice, and wasn't sure whether to rejoice or curse. She emerged from between two stacks of containers, pistol held firmly in a two-handed grip and leveled at the black-clad thug.

"New Lyons Police Department. You move, asshole, and I'll put a bullet in your brain." She looked past the man, watching me.

He hadn't turned yet; I could see his eyes, and she couldn't. Hernandez was concentrating on me, waiting for my cue on whether to pull the trigger. We needed the guy alive, but where was the sniper? I felt exposed, too exposed. I eased my pistol from its holster, leveling it at my would-be killer. "I've got him, Hernandez," I said. "We need to find some cover. There may be a guy with a rifle out—"

I didn't have time to finish the sentence.

There was no report. Just a sound like a hammer hitting a melon. I felt a wet, warm spray splash across my face and almost fired on reflex. Instead, I dove to the ground. I think I screamed for Hernandez, but everything was happening so fast that I couldn't be sure. I hit the pavement and rolled, coming to a hard stop against one of the containers. Part of my mind, the soldier part, was still working, processing. Wherever the shooter was, he had a clear shot down the alleyway, which meant that he was likely at one end or the other of the "street" created by the stacked containers.

I low-crawled backward as fast as I could, keeping my body tight to the metal and feeling my way with my feet. When I found a break in the containers, I risked a half crouch and hurled myself around the corner. It hadn't taken long, maybe five seconds, maybe ten. Long enough for a competent shooter to have gotten off at least one more round. "Hernandez?" I shouted. Stealth was out the window anyway. "You hit?"

"Fuck! No!" came the angry reply. "Whoever pulled the trigger shot the perp. He's dead."

Shit. So much for getting answers from him. "He wasn't alone," I called back. "I dropped two more. One's cuffed. The other should still be out."

"Great. Now how do we get to them without getting shot?" A pause. "My screen doesn't seem to be working."

"Mine, either." We couldn't stay where we were. The shooter knew our location and if I were him, I'd be on the move already, trying to find a better angle to take one, or both, of us out. "We have to move. I'm coming to you."

I didn't wait for her to object, but put my words to action. I wasn't, however, stupid enough to run right back out into the lane where my would-be assassin had himself been assassinated. Instead, I sprinted around the other side of the containers, my shoulder brushing the wall as I ran. I didn't know exactly where Hernandez had taken cover, but I had a general idea, and I didn't make any effort to be quiet. If the sniper wanted to get close enough where he could hear me running, then he'd be close enough for me to do something about.

"Campbell?" the hiss came from off to my left, and I turned down a narrow alley between two stacks.

"Here," I said.

"This way." It was a woman's voice, but distorted by a strained whisper.

I had one fleeting what-if moment. What if that wasn't Hernandez? What if the shooter was a woman who, in my agitated state, just sounded a little bit like Hernandez? Hell, what if Hernandez was somehow in on it all? I squashed that thought. She was a friend, and she hadn't hesitated to help, even once she knew the truth.

I turned another corner, and there she was, crouched with her back pressed against a red shipping crate and her service weapon grasped in both hands. The barrel came up, just a bit, as I came into view, but then she recognized me and let it drop down. "You've got us in some serious shit, *hermano*," she growled.

"Yeah, yeah," I grunted. "Mea culpa. Can we maybe save that for a time when we're not getting shot at?"

She chuckled at that. Actually chuckled. Pinned down by sniper fire—or at least the threat of it, operating without backup, a dead body on our hands, and very shaky ground from a legal standpoint, and she chuckled. Hernandez was a bona fide badass. "All right, Campbell," she agreed. "But what do we do now?"

I shrugged, putting my back against the wall next to hers and sliding down in a crouch. She was keeping her eyes to the left, scanning the tops of the containers, watching for any kind of movement. I did the same, keeping mine to the right. Unless the bastard managed to come up on the container behind us, we had at least a chance of seeing him moving around. "Well, I *was* going to head out to sea and swim for it. But that was before I realized I had a real chance at interrogating one of these bastards."

"How many are there?"

"At least four. The one you saw. Two more that I made go night-night. And the shooter."

The reminder of the one she saw seemed to shake her for a moment. "Why would they gun down their own man?"

"We had him," I replied. "Dead to rights. He wasn't going to get away. I guess the shooter didn't want anyone telling tales."

"Then why shoot him? Why not us?"

I thought about that for a moment. "He's smart. He knew he'd only get one good shot. Maybe he kills me. Maybe you. But the other one could still get away. And maybe keep the bad guy collared while they did it. This way, he guaranteed we wouldn't get a chance to question him."

"Shit. You know what that means, *hermano*? The two you took down..." She trailed off.

I thought a moment and then cursed. "They're probably gone or dead already. Fuck. But I have to be sure. If there's even a chance that we can talk to one of them..."

"OK. You're the former supersoldier. This shit's way out of the norm for G&G. You lead the way. And if you get me shot, so help me God, Campbell, I'm going to be pissed."

Badass.

We moved quickly, keeping low and staying in cover. When we had to leave the relative safety of our positions pressed up against the container walls, we did so at a sprint. No sparking walls or powdering concrete indicated a near miss from an observant sniper as we made our way through the steel maze. I wasn't entirely sure where my encounters with the goons had taken place—in the dark, with adrenaline pumping, and running for my life it was hard to be all that observant as to exactly which random turns I had taken. But, after a number of false starts, we made our way back to where I'd taken down the second guy.

There was nothing to be seen. A smear of drying blood where the bad guy's skull had met the steel wall of the container. A few more crimson splashes on the concrete, barely distinguishable in the darkness. That was it.

"Shit," I muttered.

"At least we didn't find a corpse," Hernandez quipped.

"We might have been able to get some information from a corpse."

"Yeah. But not without some serious investigation from Internal Affairs. I don't think we want that."

She had a point. The dead guy lying somewhere amid the maze had a bullet in his head—what was left of it, but that bullet hadn't come from a cop's gun. Bad-guy-on-bad-guy action wasn't likely to get me in any trouble, as long as I could come up with a reason for being here in the first place. Something better than "So, this synthetic was killed...."

I grunted. "Let's go find the other guy. I cuffed that bastard to a crate. He's not getting away so easily."

We kept in cover, but I had the growing impression that it wasn't necessary. My instincts told me that the shooter was gone. One bad guy dead. One disabled but missing. One shooter gone. And one that wouldn't get away easily.

"It definitely wasn't easy," Hernandez said, looking down at the pool of blood.

My cuffs were still there. One ring was closed around a metal bar on the container. The other was empty, hanging from its short length of chain. Empty, but still closed. A puddle of slowly congealing blood pooled beneath it and a spray of lines and droplets ran down the side of the container.

"Christ," I whispered. "He cut off his fucking hand."

"And then took it with him," Hernandez added, her eyes sweeping the ground around the container. "That doesn't sound like ordinary corporate thugs or mercenaries, Campbell. I can understand—maybe—taking out the guy we had the drop on to prevent us from getting any information, but this?"

She had a point. The shooter had already demonstrated his willingness to kill his own men. Taking the shot would have cost the gunman only a few seconds, and left him plenty of time to make a clean escape. But coming down here, finding the cuffed man, and freeing him? That spoke of a level of confidence and discipline that few could boast. It also hinted at a pragmatism—eliminate the unrecoverable asset and rescue the recoverable at any cost—that sent a cold shiver rolling down my spine. We hadn't even heard any screams—and we would have, unless they had timed things so perfectly that the crash of the cranes would cover them.

"What now?" Hernandez asked.

She wasn't talking about how to get out of the maze alive—not any more. She must have sensed, just as I had, that the danger was past. We could walk back to her cruiser and be on our merry way, none the wiser, but significantly less dead than our adversaries had hoped.

But that didn't account for the body with a mostly missing head lying on the concrete in the midst of the container stacks. "We have to call it in," I said with a sigh.

Hernandez nodded. Neither of us *wanted* to call it in, but we weren't spoiled for choice. Even if Hernandez was willing to walk away—and I wasn't sure either of us could do that—we didn't have that luxury. There might not have been cameras among the electromagnetic wasteland inside the dockyards, but we went through the main gate. No one would buy the notion that we just happened upon a murder victim in the midst of some other kind of investigation.

Which meant that it was going to be a long night of questions and explaining. The captain was going to want to know why a Guns and Gangs detective and a Homicide detective were working together in the first place. If she found out that we were investigating the death of a synthetic, she'd blow a gasket. And probably suspend me. And possibly Hernandez as well. I didn't want to go down that path.

Some part of me—some dark part that I was trying hard to suppress—knew that my time on the NLPD was coming to a close. But I needed the authority the badge granted me to keep going on my investigation. Without that stamp of legitimacy, I worried that the scant leads I'd managed to wrap my fingers around so far would slip through my desperate grasp, dry up, and blow away. But what about Hernandez? Would she agree to get our stories straight before calling it in?

"So," I asked, trying to hedge my way around the issue, "what's our play?"

She was still looking at the handcuffs. She was quiet for a moment; then, as if making a decision, she reached out and pressed her thumb to the release pad on the cuffs. They clicked open, and she tossed them to me. "You may want to throw those in the ocean, *hermano*," she said. "As for our play, we tell the truth." I felt a sinking in my stomach, until an evil little grin split her face. "To a point."

"And what point is that?" I asked, trying to keep the edge of nervousness from my voice.

"To the point that doesn't get us kicked off the job." She turned and started walking back toward the landward side of the container stacks. She wasn't moving in the sprinting half crouch we used before. But she *was* staying close to the metal walls. We were fairly sure the shooter was gone, but there was no need to be too careless, after all. "We tell the brass we were reviewing footage from Manny's shop, looking for new

G&G contacts. I do that from time to time anyway. Suit guy came up and looked pretty suspicious—which he did. So I went down to investigate, see if maybe Manny was branching out to new customers, or if we had tumbled onto a gang lawyer or accountant. Those are always good for a bunch of arrests, since they think they're too smart to get caught and don't ever want their lily-white asses to see the inside of a prison cell. That lead took me here, and the guy at Translantic told us to meet him here. But all we found was a body."

It was a good story. Almost too good. There were always rumors about the people on Guns and Gangs, and how their version of the law was just a little different than that of other cops. But now was not the time to start second-guessing Hernandez. Her story might satisfy the brass, except for one little detail. "And why am I here?" I asked.

"Because you pussies in Homicide never get to do any real work anymore. You were bored and lonely and wanted something to do. So I let you tag along." She shot another evil grin over her shoulder.

It was going to be a long night.

Chapter 22

Dealing with the aftermath at the docks took hours. We had backup on scene within a few minutes, but that was only the beginning. It took time to secure the area, especially when Hernandez suggested that the murderer might yet be hiding among the containers. I didn't think it likely, but alert cops were careful cops, and neither of us wanted them taking any chances—not after what we'd been through.

Fitzpatrick arrived about a half hour in, and we escorted him to the body. There wasn't much for him to do. Cause of death was clear, even if we didn't let him know that the actual murder had been witnessed by two cops. He did his thing with time of death and a cursory examination, and then had the corpse bustled onto a gurney to be taken back to his lab. An autopsy would be done—unlike with the synthetics, it was required by law in the event of a violent death. But I was pretty confident that it wouldn't find anything beyond the obvious. Our adversary, the esteemed Mr. Fowler or those who employed him, were far too careful for that.

Captain Harris arrived at the hour-and-a-half mark. She wasn't happy. She was never happy. But she liked Hernandez a hell of a lot more than she did me, so I tried to fade into the background while Hernandez spun her web of bullshit. Harris didn't like it—I could see that much from where I leaned against a cruiser. There was a lot of hand waving and angry expressions, but in the end, Hernandez gave a brisk salute and turned away. She flashed a wink at me and I knew that her story had held.

I was Homicide, and even though I was technically off duty, I was the guy on the scene. The brass might not like the idea of different units working together without their express permission, but that wink told me that the case could continue as a joint venture between Guns and Gangs and Homicide. Between Hernandez and me.

That was a small victory in a night that was, otherwise, full of defeats. The forensics teams didn't find anything near the murder site that was of any use. They did find the pool of blood where the man I'd cuffed escaped, but other than taking samples, there wasn't much to go on. Hernandez and I played dumb with respect to the blood—cuffing a perp and leaving him while going after another wasn't, strictly speaking, against policy, but when that suspect cut off his hand to escape, administrative punishment was the least of your worries.

We returned to Translantic Shipping, to find it gone. Just...gone. The building remained, of course, and most of the furniture was still within, but the screens, all the files, anything that might have stored a shred of usable data had vanished. They had probably started closing it down ten minutes after we left. By now, the company had likely been sold off or dissolved outright, with any traces leading back to Walton Biogenics long since purged. Another dead end. Another lead gone.

Hernandez and I were the last on the scene, standing by her cruiser as the last of the uniforms piled back in their vehicles and drove away. There were no crowds. Not at this hour. Not at this place. There were probably workers—synthetic workers—around somewhere, but for the moment, we were alone.

"What now?" Hernandez asked.

"I honestly don't have a fucking clue," I said, hating the bitterness that tinged my voice, but unable to keep it out. "All I have—all I've ever had—is a list of names. Victims and their possible killers. Fowler was the only lead. Fowler to Manny. Manny to Translantic. Translantic to a trap." I shook my head and cursed again. "The real pisser is, they could have covered their tracks. There was no reason to bring Manny into the loop. If Fowler—whoever the fucker really is—had his ID made at Walton instead of a known gang contact, we wouldn't even have that much."

"They did it on purpose," Hernandez agreed. "To find out if anyone tumbled onto them. So that they could silence any investigation before it had any chance to gain real traction."

"And we walked right into it. We knew it was a trap, and we walked in anyway."

"And lived," Hernandez pointed out. "Don't forget that part, *hermano*. We walked into their little trap, and we took it down. They had to flee. They left behind at least one corpse. Do you think that was what they intended? No. They aren't invincible. They aren't infallible. And, you know something, Campbell? I bet they're scared shitless right now."

She said the last bit with such satisfaction that I felt a slight chuckle escape my lips. There were stereotypes about Latinas and passion going back a long way—in Hernandez that passion seemed to have settled into a nice little vindictive streak. But Walton Biogenics, one of the richest corporations in the world, scared? It didn't seem too likely. "They know us, now, Melinda," I said softly. "Not just me. Both of us. If they set up the trap at Manny's, then they had to be monitoring it. And monitoring the Translantic office, too. We didn't just walk into their trap. We identified ourselves by name. How long will it take them to find out more about us? Sure, the department has extra security measures in place for our personal information, but how long will those walls hold up? They're almost certain to come after us."

Hernandez's face twisted in anger and contempt—not directed at me, I knew, but rather at the people who would "come after us." For a moment, I thought she was going to spit out an appropriately tough line, like "Let them try." But then her face suddenly went deathly pale. "Arlene," she said in a near whisper.

"Let's go," I said at once. Christ. They wouldn't just come after us. Not now that they had tried and failed. They'd come after our families. Hernandez's daughter. My parents. Fuck.

We got into the car and Hernandez immediately switched it to manual drive, bypassing the integrated safety features. She barked a sharp command and the light bar emerged from its recessed port atop the cruiser, blazing to life. She didn't bother with the siren—the lights would trigger a signal that would be broadcast to any nearby traffic, communicating with their navigation systems to ensure a clear path for the emergency vehicle. She'd have to report it later, justify its use, but that didn't matter at the moment.

She tore out of the parking lot, tires screeching and leaving a long line of black on the pavement behind us. As she did, she tore her screen from her pocket. "Call home," she snapped. We waited in silence as the screen rang. And rang. And rang. No answer. As she hit End, Hernandez didn't say anything, and neither did I, but her white-knuckled grip on the steering wheel spoke volumes. She concentrated on the driving, taking turns at speeds that had me bracing myself against the frame. I couldn't see the speedometer, but I guessed that on the straightaways we were climbing upwards of a hundred miles an hour.

I wasn't sure where Hernandez lived. We were work friends. She liked to keep her family separated from the job. And I had learned with Annabelle the dangers of letting anyone get too close. So I had no idea how far out we were when she started talking. "We gave them plenty of time," she said between clenched teeth. "We sat there while forensics swept the area; we sat there while the coroner took care of the body; we waited for the fucking uniforms to leave. We gave them *hours* to find out where I live. To find my daughter. To find out how to hurt me."

"No corporation ever made a decision in a couple of hours, Hernandez," I replied. "Whatever they decide to do about us, it's going to have to go through a committee or a project manager or at least a damn meeting. And it's not going to happen at one in the morning. It will be all right." I said the words, but I wasn't entirely sure that I believed them. Should I call my parents? Wake them up? Tell them to get out, now? To go somewhere, anywhere, and to do it without leaving a trail?

I chewed at the thought as Hernandez continued to drive. She didn't speak again, and didn't seem mollified. Maybe corporations did need time to make decisions, but it was entirely possible that Fowler was freelance. A contractor empowered to do whatever he had to to get the job done. Or maybe Walton Biogenics had contingency plans in case their little ambush went south. Whatever the case, it was clear Hernandez didn't put much stock in my words. I wasn't sure I did, either.

A few minutes later we came to a screeching halt in front of a little Cape Cod–style house. The yard was neatly kept, with a little wrought iron fence, no more than two and a half feet high, bordering it. The porch light was still on.

And the door was wide open.

"No." It was part whisper, part plea, part prayer. It was, perhaps, the single most heartbreaking word I had ever heard.

Hernandez didn't let her fear slow her. After that first whisper, she was out of the car, pistol in hand. I was right behind her, my weapon at the low ready. She retained enough presence of mind, or perhaps just enough training and experience, to not rush headlong through that open door. We entered in tandem, clearing sight lines and watching each other's back. I wasn't sure I could have kept the same composure had our positions been reversed.

The lights were on, though I didn't have much time for looking around. I got a sense, an impression, of a well-kept space furnished with that indefinably feminine edge that seemed to make a house feel homey and that had eluded me for so many years. The house was small: entryway, stairs leading up, kitchen visible across an open floor plan, living room.

Occupied living room.

A woman sat on the couch, her face calm. She was older, perhaps in her early forties, but still attractive in a stately way. She had honey-blond hair and wore simple khaki slacks with a button-down blouse. It had the sense of a uniform, somehow.

"Where is she?" Hernandez demanded the second she caught sight of the woman. She did not, I noted, move her pistol to cover her, obviously not considering her a threat. The nanny, then. The synthetic nanny. "Where is Arlene?"

"Gone," the woman replied in a low contralto. "Taken by a man in a nice suit."

"You didn't stop him?" she demanded.

The woman smiled, and in that smile I saw a depth of bitterness that bespoke a nightmarish existence far beyond my banal experiences of war and murder. That smile pierced me to my very soul—not, I was ashamed to admit, because it implied dark and dangerous things about our world, but because in it, I could see Annabelle. An Annabelle that had lived her life as a synthetic, subject to an eternity of torment until, at the end, there was nothing left but a soulless hulk. Until the constant cycle of pain and subjugation finally turned synthetics into that which we already claimed they were: something less than human.

The thoughts flashed through my head in an instant, but my concentration was still on the room, still on my surroundings. Still on Hernandez. The barrel of her pistol was coming up, taking bead on the center of the nanny's chest. "Melinda, no!" I barked sharply, moving quickly to interpose my body between the two.

"Why not?" To my surprise, the words were not Melinda's, but rather those of her nanny. "I've been dead for years. I wish I could end it myself, but I can't. So go ahead. I'll make it easy. I hope they do to your little girl all the things that have been done to me. All the dirty little secrets no one wants to talk about." She kept smiling.

I was facing the nanny, my back to Hernandez, but I could hear the ragged, rapid pant of her breathing. She was terrified and angry. "*Puta*," Hernandez growled. "You shouldn't even be able to think that, much less say it." The anger in her voice was deep, visceral. I'd been in that state, more than once, and I knew that rage wanted a target, hungered for it. Something to take it out on. Something to hurt. To break.

And here was a synthetic, not protected by any laws and incapable of offering any real resistance. She had to know the suffering that Hernandez could legally visit upon her, and yet she smiled. You rarely saw old synthetics. Was this why? There was a time when suicide by cop was a thing, the depressed and mentally ill forcing a standoff with the police and taking aggressive enough action that the officers had no choice but to open fire on the suspect. Did the life of a synthetic wear upon them so greatly that suicide by owner became their only option?

It hung there, balanced on a razor's edge, the cold, dead smile of the synthetic and the tension and anger and helplessness radiating off Hernandez in a palpable wave. I didn't think she'd throw me out of the way just to pull the trigger, but I was standing in the worst possible place to prevent it if she did. I needed to defuse the situation. I needed to say something.

"Do you know Silas?" I had no real reason to think that she would know the strange synthetic who had started all this. But Silas had implied some sort of organization, some sort of cohesion...almost a resistance.

At the mention of Silas's name, the frozen smile shattered.

"How do you know that name?" she demanded.

We didn't have the time for explanations. Somewhere out there, a killer had Hernandez's daughter. If he was smart, he wouldn't hurt her. Damaged goods made poor bargaining chips, after all. But the sooner we tracked him down, the better our chances of getting Arlene back in one piece. So I went for the shortest possible answer. "I'm helping him." She just stared at me blankly, as if she couldn't possibly have heard me correctly. "Silas," I said again. The name had an effect like an electric bolt upon her. She physically started every time I said it. "We are helping him, damn it. Did you see where they took Arlene? Do you know anything?"

I could still feel Hernandez's rage boiling behind me, not the least bit tempered by the shock on her nanny's face. "A car," she said at last, voice flat. "A black sedan. Fancy. They left maybe fifteen minutes ago. Caucasian. Male. Mid thirties." There was no malice in the words now, no hatred. No love or caring, either. Just an empty monotone that was, all at once, sad and terrifying.

"Call it in, Hernandez," I said without turning. I didn't want to give her a clear lane, even for the second it would take to turn. "Get the techies tracking that vehicle. Do it now, Melinda. It's our best chance."

"*Bruja*," Hernandez spat. But I heard the scrape of metal and composite as she holstered her weapon and dug out her screen.

"You should have let her kill me," the nanny said.

I sighed. "What's your name?"

"The name they called me at 'birth' was Sinthyia," she said, putting the emphasis on the *Sin*.

"What's your name?" I asked again. "What do you call yourself?"

She glared at me, as if I'd asked her to strip naked. No. If I'd asked that, she'd probably have done it, as much on reflex as anything. She glared as if I were asking her to do something far more personal. A slight glimmer of outrage mixed with challenge flashed through her dead eyes. "Thea," she almost growled. "My name is Thea."

"Well, Thea, Hernandez is one of the good ones. She's scared out of her mind at the moment, scared and angry and looking for a target."

"Yeah. Been there. Done that."

There was something in her voice that was both dismissive and defeatist and it made me want to scream. I couldn't blame her for it, not after the life I assumed she had led. But was assuming that all non-synthetics were callous assholes who would use and throw away any synthetic that crossed their path any better than what people did to the synthetics? Well. Yes. OK. It was better. But it still wasn't fair.

I almost snorted at that. Life was all kinds of things. Fair was seldom one of them.

"I know there was nothing you could do to stop Fowler," I said. "And I know why you hate us. I find it hard to believe that your hate extends so far that other little girls getting hurt would really make you feel better."

She winced at my words, but the slight flinch was all the acknowledgment I'd get. "What happens to me now?" Thea asked.

The question surprised me, and I hated myself a little bit for that flash of surprise. Hated that I could still be surprised by the notion that synthetics had a sense of self-determination and worried about the future.

"What do you mean?" I fumbled.

She snorted. "I don't think Ms. Hernandez is going to want me watching after little Arlene anymore. If she doesn't kill me, then what? Sold again, I suppose." The words were spoken pragmatically, almost stoically, but I could hear the worry in them, the fear.

Hernandez returned. "They're working on it," she said. "They'll call us if they find anything. Uniforms are inbound to go over the scene." The words were familiar—every detective had said them to colleagues, to the family of victims, or to the press hundreds of times. But the familiar words sounded different now, coming from Hernandez's mouth.

She looked past me, at her nanny. "Get out."

"What?" Thea asked.

"Get out," Hernandez repeated. "I won't sell you. Not with what I know now. But I'll be damned if I let you around my daughter ever again. So get out."

Thea stared at Hernandez. "But...where will I go? What will I do?"

"I. Don't. Care," Hernandez ground out.

It was no kindness, I realized. The nanny had no legal status, no way to earn money, no rights whatsoever. Kicking her out onto the street was as likely to be a death sentence as it was anything else.

Could I blame Hernandez? I had no doubt that Thea had lived a hard life—far harder than anyone should. I understood how that could make her hate those who claimed to be above her, to seek out any revenge that she could. But I couldn't blame Hernandez, either. This woman had done nothing as Melinda's daughter was taken.

There was no flicker of emotion in Hernandez's eyes as they bored into her nanny, still seated on the couch, looking, for the first time, scared and worried. She had been neither when Hernandez had leveled a gun at her chest. That look of fear, of hopelessness, prodded me to action. "Can you find Silas?" I asked. It was a shot in the dark, but the albino tunnel worker had hinted at a vast network of synthetics, and she had, after all, known his name.

"Maybe," she said.

"Then go to him. Tell him what happened. Tell him Detective Campbell needs his help. Tell him that we need to find the people who took Arlene. They're the same people he's looking for." If we could find them, and Fowler, maybe I could finally have some answers. "Tell him you need a place to stay." I paused, thinking. "Tell him I would consider it a favor if he helped you." I wasn't sure if that would have any weight with Silas, or if it would even be needed.

But it was all I could offer, so I did.

Chapter 23

We waited.

There really wasn't much else we could do. Kidnappings were new territory for me. In addition to being another crime that had seen a remarkable decline with the advent of synthetics—though custody-related kidnaps still happened from time to time—it was generally the territory of the feds. They showed up, of course, men and women staying true to the stereotype with their dark suits and humorless expressions. Neither Hernandez nor Mel had called them, but it was procedure. It would have been one of the first things someone down at the precinct would have done. It was a bad idea—mostly—to have cops involved in investigations into their own, or those involving their families.

That didn't stop most of the NLPD from showing up, of course. Hernandez's fellow officers from Guns and Gangs came out in force. Not just those from our precinct, but from all around the city. Captain Harris showed up, her uniform looking as pressed and pristine as ever. Other officers—some I knew, some I'd never even seen—until the entire place was beginning to resemble some sad shadow of a policeman's ball.

The show of support should have been reassuring. It wasn't. We'd been doing far too much lying with respect to this case for it to be anything other than nerve wracking for me. How long before the truth came out and all these officers realized this happened because I refused to stop investigating the deaths of synthetics? Endangering another officer's family—even indirectly—through that particular activity was sure to spell the end of my career. I was surprised to find that the thought of my looming unemployment didn't really bother me much. If I could get Arlene back and find the scumbag who had been butchering synthetics, then the rest of the job could go fuck itself.

"A moment, Detective?"

I looked up from my reverie to find a dark-suited man with a crew cut staring back at me. One of the feds, no doubt. "Yeah?"

"We need to get your statement."

I knew this had been coming. A pair of feds had taken Hernandez off into another room, while the tech weenies started working whatever voodoo they worked with her personal screen and the various screens throughout the house. "Right. What do you need?"

"Just tell me what happened. I'm Agent Thornton, by the way." He offered his hand, and I shook it. He was shorter than me, stocky. Close up, I could see that his crew cut probably had as much to do with his thinning hair as it did any desire to keep up the image.

"Detective Hernandez and I were following up on an inconsistency at a local forger. That interview led us to the docks, where we discovered a body." And got shot at. I left that part out. "We returned here to find the door kicked open and Detective Hernandez's daughter missing. The nanny, a synthetic, was unable to provide any meaningful information beyond the vehicle description we called in and the fact that she was taken by a white male."

"Right," Thornton said. "And where is this nanny now?"

"Out." My response was brusque, almost terse. It earned me a raised eyebrow. "Look," I said, "Detective Hernandez was not happy, all right? Her daughter had just been taken. And the nanny hadn't done anything to stop it. Couldn't have, anyway, right? Synthetics being incapable of harming...humans." I had almost let slip an "others" amid that, as in other humans, but managed to keep it in. "It seemed like a good idea to send her off on an errand, to give Detective Hernandez a chance to cool down. I doubt she'll be back for several hours." Actually, I was fairly certain she would never come back.

I couldn't tell if the fed was buying it, but I left it at that. He just nodded and moved on to the next question. It was a fairly routine interview, with none of the repetitive questions designed to catch the other guy in a lie. That was a small mercy—and professional courtesy, one cop to another. Thornton was wrapping up when my screen beeped.

"Excuse me," I said, waiting for his slight nod before walking away.

I dug the screen out of my pocket as I went, and glanced down at the display. The number was listed as unavailable, and it was a voice-only call. I hit the Answer button and raised the screen to my ear. "Campbell."

"Detective." I didn't recognize the voice. Male, possessed of neither the exuberance of youth nor the feebleness of age. A smooth baritone that oozed confidence and self-assurance.

"Yeah?"

"It is imperative that you answer me honestly. Doing anything else will result in the death of the young miss." My blood ran cold at the words. I probably should have flagged down the nearest fed, but something in that voice, that too-smooth voice, assured me that doing so would be the death of Arlene Hernandez. "Have the federal agents or the New Lyons police put any additional monitoring devices or programs on your screen?" the voice continued. "Beyond those that are standard for any officer?"

"No," I replied.

"Are you currently in a position where this conversation can be overheard?"

I glanced around the house. There were people everywhere, but they were still in the initial stage of doing that always preceded the long and arduous stage of waiting. Waiting for the call that I was currently on. They were all too distracted to be listening in. "Possible," I admitted. "But unlikely."

"Good. Listen very carefully, Detective. You have poked your nose in where it does not belong. And you've had the bad manners to get Detective Hernandez involved as well, which I am certain she is deeply regretting."

I felt more than a twinge of guilt at that. The danger that Hernandez was in was my fault.

"But I am a kind man," he continued. "So I will give you this one opportunity to set things right. What I propose is a simple trade. You come to an address I will provide, alone. And when I say alone, Detective, I do mean it. You'll be monitored from the moment you leave the Hernandez residence. When you arrive, I will release the child. You will then accompany me and we will talk about certain matters."

"You mean you'll kill me," I replied. I managed to say the words flatly, without any real inflection, though I couldn't deny the tremor of fear coursing through me.

"I genuinely hope not, Detective. I will, of course, if it comes to that. But I would much prefer not to." There was a brief pause. "Don't get me wrong. If you had died at the docks, this all would have been much easier, but that event could have been written off as some sort of gang-related violence. We're past that now. If you were to turn up dead, it would be messy, and might cause undue attention. My employers *will* risk that attention, if there's no other option. But I'm hoping we can find another way."

Not terribly fucking likely. Whatever Mr. Fowler—if that was the asshole on the other end of the call—said, I was pretty sure the endgame was a shallow grave for Momma Campbell's favorite boy. I smiled into the phone. "When and where?"

* * * *

Getting out wasn't easy. At times like this, there were only two acceptable modes for officers—out kicking the ass of whoever messed with one of our own, or at their side providing support. I *was* going out to try to get Arlene back, but I couldn't let any of the officers around me know that. Or Hernandez. Which put me in an awkward spot.

I managed a few minutes with Hernandez, and let her know that I was going to try to find Silas and see what he knew. That had been my plan, before Fowler's call. But I couldn't tell the captain, or any of the other NLPD, and certainly not the feds, about Silas. Or Fowler. Or any damn thing that would be helpful. At least not without putting the girl at risk. And if I so much as hinted to Hernandez that I had a shot at getting her daughter—or the guy that nabbed her—there was no force on earth that could have stopped her from coming with me. So I just sort of...left.

I'd catch hell for it later. You didn't walk out on a crime scene, particularly one the feds had taken control of, without so much as a by-your-leave. But I figured that no matter how this night ended, my career was over anyway. I couldn't go back to pretending that the bodies dropping in the streets weren't human, that the assaults and abuses were all A-OK because, after all, synthetics were just *things*. I couldn't go back to enforcing the laws that allowed it to happen.

But I needed to find Fowler. I needed to find out what the hell was going on with the missing women—the eviscerated women. And most of all, I needed to get Hernandez's daughter back. Even if it meant trading my life for hers.

We'd arrived in Hernandez's car, which was a problem. Mine was still back at the precinct, and I couldn't take one of the cruisers parked outside. They'd respond to me well enough, but my location would be logged, and Central could send an abort-and-return order to the vehicle at any time.

So I started walking.

I'd catch a cab, but didn't want to do that right in front of Hernandez's house, either. Better if people thought I might still be hanging around somewhere. A cab would be noticed. I went about two blocks before I finally pulled out my screen and called for a car. I did it the old-fashioned way, typing in an address from the nearest house rather than letting them sniff my GPS coordinates. I couldn't disable that feature of my screen—that would trigger all kinds of alarms with the tech guys—so after I ordered the cab, I shut the device off entirely and waited.

I didn't have long to wait. The car, a two-seater electric box barely half the size of my police-issued cruiser, pulled to the curb maybe five minutes later. It was painted bright yellow and the company's name, URide, stood out in bold black letters. There was no driver, of course. Cabs had gone fully automated years ago, long before driverless cars became mainstream for the rest of the population. I popped the passenger door and sank into the chair. Once I'd shut the door and engaged the safety belt, the cab immediately pulled away from the curb.

I wasn't familiar with the address Fowler had provided, so I hit the Navigation button on the dash. A map of the city appeared on the windshield, outlining the route and highlighting my current position. Traffic information, speed limits, places of interest along the way, all of them blossomed to life alongside the blue line. A few quick swipes and I had isolated the destination—and isolated was the operative word. It wasn't all that far in terms of absolute distance. I'd arrive in about twenty minutes.

The location rested in the heart of an old commercial district that had seen nothing but decline over the past ten or fifteen years. As I got closer, the tidy strip malls and grocery stores thinned, giving way first to ill-kept thrift and liquor shops and, eventually, to abandoned and boarded-up storefronts. By the time the cab neared its final destination, even those had thinned, leaving me in the middle of concrete wasteland.

I'd seen few enough people along the way—some homeless despite the government stipend, some desperately holding on to a crumbling house or store. A few dealers lingering on street corners. No one who looked like they'd give two damns if I got myself murdered, particularly if they knew I was a cop.

The cab stopped in a parking lot in front of an abandoned commercial complex. All the signs were long gone, all the windows broken. It had probably been thriving twenty years earlier, but fewer and fewer people bothered leaving the comfort of their homes for something as mundane as shopping. Brick-and-mortar stores had been a dying breed for a long time, now, but in this part of New Lyons, they seemed a little more serious about it.

I scanned the lot, but I didn't see any other vehicles. I already knew that Fowler had a penchant for long-range shooting, and there were plenty of perches that would afford a wonderful view of the parking lot. But the cab would grant me little enough protection if he was sitting somewhere with a high-caliber weapon. I was committed. I hit the button that told the cab to wait there and keep the meter running—it would sit as long as there was juice in the batteries and credit in my accounts. Then I climbed out of the car.

As I closed the door behind me, my fingers itched to hold the butt of my service weapon. I refrained from drawing it, though. If Fowler was out there with a rifle, that would be the perfect cue for him to open fire. Arlene couldn't afford that kind of mistake. Instead, I waited, standing by the car and trying to be as nonchalant as possible, despite the sudden, nearly overwhelming desire to be moving, doing. Something. Anything.

Across the parking lot, from deep in the shadows between two derelict buildings, a pair of headlights flashed.

The brief flash of light revealed an alleyway that hadn't been visible in the gloom. It also sent my heart rate into overtime and my hand flashing toward my gun. I controlled both impulses as best I could, and forced myself to take a deep breath. I turned and made my way, one slow step at a time, across the open expanse of concrete and toward the other vehicle. If Fowler—assuming it was Fowler—wanted me dead, he couldn't have chosen a better setup. The abandoned lot left me with nowhere to run or hide. And the alleyway provided him an excellent view over all of it. Even if he managed to miss with a shot or two, he'd have plenty of time to spray and pray before I had any hope of finding cover. Every instinct I'd developed as a soldier, as a cop, screamed at me to turn back, to take cover. Arlene was probably dead already, and throwing my life away would not only fail to bring her back, it would also ensure that the Walton Biogenics cover-up continued. It was pure idiocy to move into that alleyway.

I kept walking.

Chapter 24

Every ounce of sense and self-preservation called at me to pull my weapon, to be ready to fight or run. I ignored it and did my level best to walk casual. The alleyway was dark, the high walls on either side blocking out the streetlights. The faint moonlight managing to trickle in from above did little to illuminate anything. My eyes were still adjusting, but about halfway down, I could make out the front end of a black sedan.

A scrape and a flash of light nearly made me jump. I realized half a heartbeat later that it was a chemical match flaring to life. The flickering orange lit up a face, as it moved to the tip of a cigarette. I recognized the face. It belonged to the man from the surveillance video outside of Manny's Barber Shop. White, middle aged, strong. Sort of distinguished. A remarkable face, really. The face of a killer.

"That's far enough, Campbell," the man said, taking a long drag from the cigarette.

"Mr. Fowler, I presume?"

"One name among many," he said with a curling exhale of smoke.

"Where's the girl?"

"In a moment. I have some questions for you first."

I grit my teeth, but there wasn't much I could do. "Ask."

"How did you find me?"

"You left a trail."

His smile was practiced. False. "I left a half dozen or so trails, Campbell. I'm curious which one you found."

"Manny's Barber Shop. Why leave trails?" I didn't know if he'd bother answering, but I figured I'd slip the question in anyway.

"The documents. I thought so, given that you've been calling me Fowler. Still, it's good to know for sure. To answer your question, I lay the false trails so I know who is looking for me. None of them are terribly hard to find, once someone starts digging. But that's the point. Part of what I'm paid to do is find those who are willing to look too closely into our blissful little utopia." The bastard actually dropped a slow, lazy wink at me. Something about it felt wrong, like it was a gesture learned rather than felt.

"So you know?" I asked. I needed to find out where Arlene was, what this asshole had done with her. But I needed answers, too.

"About the so-called synthetics? Of course I know. I wonder, though, if you do."

"And you kill them? Gut them? Why?"

He laughed. A chill ran down my spine. I wasn't sure if that chill was because the man before me was himself something truly less than human... or if it was because he personified all that we had become, a callous, narcissistic, self-indulgent husk lacking any capacity for true empathy.

"Because I can, of course. Oh, also for money. Walton Biogenics pays me very well to keep their dirty laundry out of sight. And they provide me with a steady list of people to remove. But I would do it anyway. And, as far as the law is concerned, it's all perfectly legal." His smile now was positively beatific.

"Kidnapping isn't. Trying to kill members of the New Lyons Police Department isn't."

Fowler shrugged. "Well, you can't be good *all* the time. And part of the fun is the thought that you might get caught."

The man, I realized, was a complete sociopath. He wasn't just some corporate cleanup man, out to sweep Walton's mistakes under the rug. He was a bona fide psychopath, a serial killer. Who had found a nine-to-five job doing what he did best. How fucked up had our society become that, from a strictly legal standpoint, he had not even managed to commit a felony—that I knew of, anyway—until taking a shot at me? And this was the man who had taken Arlene.

"Where's the girl?" I asked.

He ignored the question. "You're not the first, you know. Not the first to pick up a trail. To start looking into the strange disappearances. The deaths. Most of the others were corporate types. In-house investigators trying to find out what happened to their property." He said the word "property" with noticeable relish, rolling it around in his mouth like a fine wine.

"The girl?" I demanded again.

"You're the first cop, though. Most of the others, they dropped it as soon as they hit the first stumbling block. In a very few cases, Walton Biogenics reached out and offered to replace the 'lost or stolen' goods in the name of excellent customer service." His smile had taken on a dark, predatory cast. "I've been pleasantly surprised at the sport you've offered, Campbell. Though I understood better once I accessed your records."

My records? That sent another little chill through me. I didn't like the idea of this psycho poring over whatever files were out there on me. Most of the good bits were supposed to be expunged or, at the very least, highly classified, but my time in the military had taught me just how little that could mean. Still, I needed to stay focused. "Where is Arlene, Fowler?"

"I think," Fowler said, continuing to ignore me, "that deep down you want to be a hero. Or maybe even a martyr. You have a long list of awards, citations, and medals from your military career. And there was that business in Vegas, of course. Did you think that was what being a cop would be like? Shootouts with the bad guys? How has that worked out for you?"

It hadn't worked out that way at all, but damn it, I was glad. All I'd ever done was what I felt I had to do, what I thought anyone with half a heart and a drop of courage would at least try. I'd gotten lucky. I'd survived. I knew a dozen men and women who hadn't. They were heroes, not me. And I had no intention of being anyone's martyr. I sure as hell wasn't going to let anyone else—like Arlene—be one, either. "The girl?" I demanded.

"Did they teach you that at the academy? The broken record technique? Ask the same question over and over until you get an answer." He laughed, a mocking little chuckle. "Speaking of little girls, maybe we should talk about Annabelle."

The air left my body in a whoosh and my gun was in my hand before I knew it, leveled at Fowler. It took every ounce of control I could muster to not pull the trigger. My arms trembled with the strain, making the sight picture jump and waver. I drew a steadying breath, and got the weapon under control. I hadn't meant to get to this point, but now that I was here, damned if I wasn't going to do it right. "Where is Arlene?" I barely recognized the growl as my own voice.

"Touchy, touchy," Fowler chided. He hadn't flinched when I pulled the gun, hadn't reacted in any way. I'd had more than a few guns pointed at me over the years, and no matter how well you hid it, there was always fear. But I didn't see any in Fowler. The man really was insane. "You really should put that down. After all, if you kill me here—no matter how satisfying you might find it—you'll never find the darling little Arlene." He paused, and tapped at a lip thoughtfully. "Well, you'll find her *eventually,* I suppose. The smell might be a bit much by then."

I ground my teeth and my gun wavered. Images flashed through my mind: Hernandez's daughter locked in the trunk of a car, in a freezer, buried alive. Suffocating. Freezing. Starving. And Fowler, the bastard, was right. Unless he had screwed up somewhere along the line, we'd never find her in time. I had come here intending to trade my life for Arlene's, but I'd at least expected to set her in the cab before Fowler pulled the trigger. He had found a way to deny me even that much.

There was a piece in Fowler's hand now. When had he drawn that? It was a sleek job, a .32, probably German. A gentleman's gun. Just as likely to do the job as the blocky forty-five in my fist. He made a sort of clicking noise with his teeth, flicking the barrel of his pistol suggestively toward the ground. The meaning was clear.

I was out of options. I had no cards left to play. And my only assurance of Arlene's safety was the dubious word of a madman. It was a slim chance. But it was the only chance Arlene had.

I knelt down and placed my pistol on the pavement.

Chapter 25

That same smug smile still pulled at Fowler's lips. "Your backup piece as well. And don't bother telling me you don't have one. Your files were quite...extensive."

I was getting extremely tired of how much Fowler seemed to know about me. I guess corporate money really could buy anything—even access to Annabelle, to records that should have been not just sealed, but destroyed. I pulled the subcompact 9mm from its ankle holster and dropped it down beside my forty-five.

"Good, Campbell. If you'd be so kind as to kick those away, we can get this wrapped up."

That didn't sound ominous at all. My mind raced as I stood back up, kicking the firearms toward some point between me and Fowler, but I kept coming up empty. I could rush him, maybe survive, maybe take him into custody. But Arlene wasn't here. And I doubted I could break him through normal interrogation.

Resigned to my fate, I lifted my face to stare my killer in the eye. His expression, that smug smile of victory, didn't change as he began to take up slack on the trigger. "Good-bye, Mr. Campbell. It's been fun."

It might be cliché, but time slowed down. I swear I could see, despite the distance, his finger edging ever closer to the break point that would send the firing pin crashing into the cartridge, igniting the primer and ending my life. Just as I saw, entering in from my peripheral vision, a spinning, shining object that smashed into Fowler's gun hand just as the shot rang out. Time came crashing back to full speed as a new voice cried out, "Take him, Detective!"

I recognized that resonant baritone as belonging to Silas. But I was already moving. Charging straight at a man with a gun was suicidal.

Whatever Silas had thrown, it knocked Fowler's gun hand off to my left. So I angled to my right, hurling myself forward, not directly toward Fowler, but at a forty-five-degree angle to him. His gun arm was sweeping back on line, already barking fire as he pulled the trigger again and again. The second my foot hit the ground, I moved back toward him, cutting in on a new line, taking me inside the sweep of his arm. I pushed both my arms in front of me, and they slammed into Fowler's gun arm.

He was still firing, the sharp report of gunfire cracking off the alley walls. At the same time, his left hand came sweeping across in an open-palmed strike, aiming for my ear. He never got the chance to land it. My right hand curled under his gun arm, finding the back of his triceps. At the same time, my left hand pushed up, angling the weapon, still firing, well over my head. Fowler's own momentum provided all the force I needed turn the man almost completely around, while simultaneously tangling his left arm with his right.

Both my hands shot forward again, sliding down his gun arm until they reached the hand, clamping down around the meat of his palm. I twisted, turning the hand back toward Fowler. At the same time, my knee smashed into the back of his thigh, destabilizing his balance. The pressure on his wrist, combined with the loss of balance, proved too much, and we both toppled toward the ground.

Hitting mats in the gym was nothing like landing on concrete. Fortunately, I managed to position Fowler between me and the ground. There was a disturbing *pop* from his wrist as my body weight fell on him, and the pistol tumbled free of his grip. He wasn't done fighting, though. While my focus had been laser-like on his gun hand, he hadn't forgotten he had another one to bring to the fight. Flashbulbs went off in front of my eyes as his left elbow smashed into the side of my head.

He was at a bad angle to throw it—if he hadn't been, it probably would have been the end of it. As it was, the shot knocked me sideways, giving him the opportunity to roll out from under me and plant himself firmly in a top mount position. I had landed on top of something angular and unyielding when I'd rolled—Fowler's pistol, presumably. But I couldn't worry about that, as Fowler began to rain blows down at me with his injured right arm. Of more concern, however, was his left hand, which darted to his pocket.

I kept my own arms active, shedding the fumbling strikes from Fowler's injured gun hand. But my eyes were more focused on his *other* hand, which, sure enough, produced a small tactical folder. The knife must have had some sort of fast-deploy feature, because even as he yanked it from his pocket, the blade—three inches of razor-edged steel—flicked open. He held it awkwardly in his left hand, grip reversed so the tip pointed down at me. He plunged the blade down *Psycho*-style.

I managed to interpose my left arm—forearm to forearm, not flesh to steel—but the moment we contacted, he pulled back, slicing the edge across my arm. I cried out as the blade cut the back of my arm, and thick, hot blood welled out. He stabbed down again and again. I managed to keep the tip from finding my face or chest, but each strike left a shallow gash along my arms. None were serious; none were even deep enough to cause any real muscle damage. But they were all bleeding, and I had only so much blood to give.

Fowler cursed. "She'll die for this, you bastard. More. She'll *suffer*. The things I did to those synthetics? I'll do far worse to that little girl. And it will be your fault."

Where was Silas? Why wasn't he helping? Could he even help, or had his programming—his brainwashing—rendered him senseless? "Fuck you, Fowler," I grunted in what was, admittedly, not my wittiest reply. "You're a fucking animal. You need to be put down."

He growled and slammed the knife down harder...but with an almost predictable rhythm. We'd been on the ground for only a few seconds, but every strike he dropped was moving across his body, pulling to my left. As he drove the knife down again, I stopped trying to block it. Instead, I threw both of my arms off to the right, creating a triangle in front of me. His knife arm struck and slid down that barrier of my arms. As it slipped past my right hand, gliding ever closer to my body, I pulled my right hand back, catching the inside of Fowler's elbow and causing his arm to fold. My left hand shot out, cupping over the top of his hand, and shoved.

His arm folded inward, the point of the knife sinking into his abdomen far on the right side. His eyes widened as the blade punched through his flesh. The shocked expression became a scream as I yanked sideways, dragging the blade across his belly and opening a nine-inch gash that went from liver to spleen.

It was messy. Beyond messy. A river of blood spurted from his lacerated liver, and blue-and-pink loops of entrails spilled from the wound. The fetid stench of shit mixed with the copper of blood—whether from a punctured bowel or from Fowler losing control over his sphincter, I didn't know. Given our relative positions, the blood and viscera—and worse—poured out directly onto me.

I gagged at the smell, grunted, heaved, and managed to roll my hips enough to escape from under the still weakly struggling Fowler. I struggled to my feet, trying to ignore the pain from the multiple gashes in my arms and the cocktail of stink assaulting my nose. I managed the former, but failed in the latter, and had to stumble to the nearest wall where I promptly lost everything I had eaten in the last week. When I finally managed to straighten again, wiping a hand stained with what I hoped was my own blood across my lips, Silas was there.

"Thanks for the help, big guy," I grunted, not feeling particularly charitable. "And for likely getting Hernandez's daughter killed."

"My apologies, Detective."

Something in the synthetic's voice made me look at him—really *look* at him. Silas looked like shit. A feverish flush suffused his too-pale skin. Beads of sweat stood out on his face, and his mouth was twisted into a moue of nausea. His hands—those big, blocky, dangerous-looking hands—were actually trembling. In fact, his entire body was trembling, almost shaking, with some sort of tremendous effort. But effort at what?

"I'm afraid I rendered all of the assistance I could when I threw the wrench." His face twisted even more at the words and for a moment, the shaking got worse.

Synthetics couldn't hurt people. I knew that. Everyone knew that. It was a security measure, a last-ditch fail-safe to ensure...product safety...but I didn't know what happened to a synthetic who *tried* to hurt someone. After all, it wasn't supposed to be possible. Their programming—indoctrination—was supposed to make it a moot point.

Silas had clearly been able to overcome that indoctrination, at least a little. And had paid the price for it. I didn't have any idea how Walton did it, but the conditioned response to violating the proscriptions against violence looked a hell of a lot like a bad case of influenza.

"Shit," I muttered. "Are you going to be all right? And how the hell did you do that in the first place?"

His massive shoulders rose and fell in something that was half shrug, half shudder. "Let's just say that anything that can be ingrained into the psyche can be overcome, or at least mitigated, provided one is willing to subject themselves to it and deal with the consequences." He smiled, though the effort of doing so was writ large on his face. "As for my injuries, you are the one bleeding, Detective."

"Fair point." I looked down at my shredded arms. My jacket was darkened and matted with blood, and felt clingy and sticky against my arms. I flexed my fingers, which sent little crackling tingles of pain from my elbows to my wrists, but everything seemed to be doing more or less what I told it to. "I'll live," I said with a shrug.

"Yes, I suppose you will. And if we hurry, so might Arlene Hernandez."

Chapter 26

Fowler was dead.

I was neither surprised nor particularly saddened by this development. But I needed to be sure. I also took the time to do a quick search of his car. I didn't expect to find Arlene stashed in the backseat or locked in the trunk, but I also wasn't taking any chances. I paused to pick up my sidearm and backup piece, checking to make sure they hadn't sustained any damage from their ignominious trip across the alleyway. Then I turned back to Silas. It had taken only moments to verify that Fowler had checked out and that his car was clear, but in that time, the big synthetic had managed to steady himself somewhat. "You ready?" I asked.

"When you are, Detective."

We made our way back to the cab. "Get in. And start talking."

Silas slumped into the passenger seat and I did the same on the nominal driver's side. "Do you know where the girl is?" I asked, before either of us had a chance to get comfortable. Covered in blood meant that getting comfortable was out the window. I must have looked like a fucking nightmare. And smelled worse. I punched the keys to lower the windows and blast the heater. The night wasn't cold enough to warrant it, but I wanted the sensation of air flowing past me. It didn't do anything for the stench, but it at least let me trick my brain into thinking it helped. I'd had quite enough vomiting for one evening.

"Perhaps, Detective."

I ground my teeth and longed for a steering wheel around which to wrap my fists. As things stood, I had a strong urge to wrap them around Silas's throat. "You better have more than fucking 'perhaps,' Silas," I grated.

"An address, Detective. I've not been idle while you've been conducting your investigation. I believe I found the location where the late, unlamented Mr. Fowler performs his...operations." He rattled off a street address, which I quickly punched into the cab. GPS indicated nearly a thirty-minute drive to reach the destination. That set my stomach churning afresh, but there was nothing I could do about it.

The car pulled from the curb and I settled back into my chair, drawing a breath. As I released it, I felt some of the tension drain from me. Fowler was dead. Arlene was still missing, but at least there was a chance I could get her back alive. I didn't delude myself into thinking it was over, or even close to over. Fowler was a tool. Walton Biogenics was the hand wielding him. But at least I could be relatively certain that no one else would try to kill me tonight. And I could be damn certain that I wasn't just going to *let* it happen.

I needed medical attention. Sleep. Food. I needed to make sure a little girl got home to her mother. And I needed answers. The only one I could do anything about at the moment was the answers.

"How did you find Fowler?" I asked Silas. "For that matter, how did you find me?"

The broad synthetic looked almost comical crammed into the small seat of the cab. He had recovered both his composure and aplomb, however, and, despite the absurdity of his position, managed to retain even the odd air of dignity that seemed so integral to who he was. "I did not find Fowler, Detective," he replied. "I did not find the girl—at least not the girl you're looking for—either."

I felt my ire start rising again. I needed to get Arlene home. "Then what did you find?"

"A different girl. Another lost soul who I believe fell into Fowler's hands." He paused a moment, reddish eyes staring intently at me. "But it stands to reason that the other detective's daughter will be there as well. If not, perhaps we can find something to lead us to her."

"Us? You dropped a list of names in my lap and disappeared. When did it become us?"

"I have been helping you all along, Detective, whether you realize it or not. Ask yourself, would it truly have been helpful to have me at your side? Would that have made your investigation any easier?" We both knew the answer to that one. "No, Detective. I gave you the information I had so that you might pursue leads that I could not. In the meantime, I have been doing the same, through channels to which your access would be extremely limited. Now that the time to act has come, I will help you directly." A grimace twisted his face. "As best I can, given the conditions under which I must operate."

I wanted to ask him again how he had overcome his conditioning, how he had managed to willfully cause harm to another person. He had hinted at practice. Practicing overcoming any of his programming, or specifically practicing doing harm? But could I blame him if it was the latter? Instead, I said, "Not good enough, Silas. I need to know where we're going. How did you even know there was another girl out there?"

He sighed. "You will not let this rest?"

"Rest?" I snorted. "I'm covered in blood and shit, may well lose some of the use of my arm, and, if I'm very, very lucky, I'll only be fired for what's gone down tonight. Rest is pretty goddamned far from my mind right now. Who's the girl? How did you find her? How did you find Fowler?"

"I have been using you, Detective. A fact, I think, of which we are both aware?" There was a question in his voice, and I snorted again. No shit. "I needed you to find a killer, and I gave you a list of victims to aid in that. You used the victims to find the killer. I used the killer to try to find his next victims. The same problem, Detective, but approached from differing ends."

That almost made sense. Identifying a pool of potential victims was a valid investigative technique, but it was more to build a profile of the perp. You couldn't use it to pick a single likely target out of the herd. Or at least, I couldn't. "Not good enough, Silas."

He was silent for a moment, long enough that I almost prodded him again. "Well, I suppose you have to learn the truth, eventually. I am not entirely alone in my undertaking, Detective. There is a network of those like me, synthetics who understand that they are not less than human, and deserve to have the same rights, the same respect, as everyone else. We do not have a name or a true leadership or anything like that—not yet. Our group is fledgling, nebulous, more an idea than a reality at this point. But we share information. Not only what we see, but what we are told by other synthetics."

I nodded, considering. He had implied as much before, when first we'd met. "How did that lead you to Fowler?"

"I told you, Detective, it didn't. But a day ago, a young synthetic woman we had been sheltering was taken. Those sheltering her..." He paused, drew a breath. "They were executed. They were synthetics, and could not do even as much as I did to help you, you understand? Killed in cold blood, without even the chance at self-defense. But the young woman was abducted. This was brought to my attention and I started tracking her down. Fowler was good, Detective, very good at what he did. And yet, I think your investigation rattled him. He was sloppy. He did an adequate job of avoiding the cameras." I heard a bit of disdain in that admission, and remembered that Silas himself was almost preternatural in his ability to stay invisible to the omnipresent electronic eyes. "Adequate, but not perfect. I followed his vehicle—electronically, you understand. I lost it, often. But with the help of some others of my ilk, we pieced together a reasonable estimation of where the vehicle stopped for the longest period of time."

"And that's where we're headed?"

"That is where we are headed, Detective."

I thought about it for a moment. My mind was spinning, maybe from the crushing weight of events over the past few days, maybe from the blood loss. Every time I turned around, I seemed to be tripping over a new conspiracy. Gutted synthetics left lying in the streets. Walton Biogenics and their fucking corporate hit squads. Silas and his band of synthetic freedom fighters. I'd been beaten, stabbed, gotten the daughter of one of my few friends kidnapped by a psychopath, and was sure as shit going to get fired, and maybe prosecuted. I wanted to scream. Instead I asked, "How did you find me? And why did you find *me*?" I placed a not-so-subtle emphasis on the last word.

He smiled, one of the few real smiles I'd ever seen cross Silas's face. It was a surprisingly warm expression, and for a moment the mystery and dignity were shattered and he sat before me as just another man, just another person. "The first was easy, Detective. I bugged you." He said the words with such delicious irony that I couldn't help the chuckle that escaped my lips. I should have been enraged at the invasion of my privacy, but given that privacy was something completely and utterly denied to synthetics—even in their own person—I couldn't manage to muster any outrage. "Before I ever came to your apartment. The cybersecurity of the New Lyons Police Department is somewhat laughable."

That should have bothered me, but at that stage? Fuck it. "Fine. Why me, Silas?"

The smile fell from his face. "Did you know that there are those out there among your kind advocating for us? On a daily basis, they stand up and say that we deserve more, that we're as human as you, or them?" I thought about the news clip on the SynthFirst lawsuit and nodded. "And they're dismissed as crackpots. Reactionaries. Bleeding hearts blinded to fact and reality." There was another moment of silence, and I saw another new emotion flicker across Silas's face. Guilt. "They cannot be our voice," he said at last.

"Because they're too easy to paint as radicals. Too easy to dismiss," I said. It wasn't a question.

"Yes."

"And then there's me," I said, a sinking feeling in the pit of my stomach. "A decorated war hero," Silas acknowledged. "A law enforcement officer. A seeker of truth. A man whose integrity is above reproach." There was a longer pause. "A man who once killed over the mistreatment of one of ours." "God damn it, Silas," I said. "And god damn you."

"Very possible, Detective."

With those ominous words, he lapsed into silence and turned his face away. Shit. Silas didn't want me to help with his budding revolution. He didn't want me to assist from the inside. He wanted me to lead it, or at least to be its face. The trusting representative of "the man," the ultimate insider turned by all things right and just and good and... "Fuck," I muttered again. If I came through this unincarcerated, I knew I was going to do it, had to do it, to make up for all the time I'd been standing still, trying to be a rock against the torrential current that was society. It was time to lean in, and put one foot in front of the other. But still...fuck.

It was clear that Silas didn't want to talk about it anymore, and I was too damn tired to push. There was nothing I could do about my wounds—the blood on the sleeves of my coat had already begun congealing anyway, forming a makeshift bandage from the tattered cloth. It was likely to tear open the minute I had to move with any real vigor, and I didn't even want to think about the probability of infection, but it was the best I had. I checked my weapons again, more out of nervous habit than any real need. Then, out of things to keep me busy, I sank back in the chair and tried very hard not to fall asleep.

* * * *

"Wake up, Detective."

The soft words pulled me from the depths of slumber. It took me a moment to process my surroundings, to remember that I was in a cab headed to find Hernandez's daughter. As that thought crashed home, it occurred to me that I hadn't called in Fowler's death—that I hadn't even considered calling it in. Had I been too wrapped up in events? Or had I truly drifted that far from who I was? Had I crossed into the bounds of a criminal?

The gunshots had undoubtedly been reported, filed away somewhere by the network of security cameras and microphones blanketing the city. Eventually, the body would be discovered. A cursory investigation would put me at the scene. If I found Arlene, it wouldn't matter, not as much. I could play it off, could plead exigent circumstances and claim that a child at risk was more important than following proper procedure. It would work. It was even true. But I wasn't completely convinced that it was *why* I hadn't called in Fowler's death.

I pushed those thoughts aside. We were here, wherever here might have been. I rubbed at my eyes—wincing as dried blood pulled at my various cuts and lacerations—forcing the last blurry vestiges of sleep from them. Here, it turned out, was a pretty damn nice neighborhood. The house was a majestic structure, all columns and balconies and black-iron fencing. It had the air of an ancient plantation home, though all the original ones were destroyed decades ago. A re-creation, then, but one done with loving attention to detail.

"I guess being a corporate hit man pays pretty good," I said as the cab came to a stop. I didn't bother putting it on standby—if things went the way I hoped, we were walking out of that house with four people, and the little two-seater taxi wasn't going to be big enough to do the job. If they didn't go as I hoped...well, I was probably going to picked up by my brothers and sisters in blue anyway. "Let's go."

I should have called for backup. It would have been the smart thing to do. The ambush at the docks—had it been just a few hours ago?—suggested that even if Fowler wasn't directly working with anyone, he, or at least Walton Biogenics, wasn't above hiring a few thugs to help out with the scut work. Silas had already proven a willingness to help if things got messy, but that willingness was trumped by his conditioning. If the shit hit the fan, I got the feeling he'd be good for about one shot, and then he'd be curled up in a ball. Not his fault, but not terribly helpful, either.

I didn't call, though. I was so far off the reservation that at best I would get a stand-down order while the brass at multiple agencies tried to figure out what the hell to do with me. It could take hours to sort out, get a SWAT or HRT team on-site, and actually gain entry to the house. I didn't think Arlene had that kind of time. So I slid my pistol from its holster and, keeping it at the low ready, advanced toward the door. Silas, silent as a ghost despite his bulk, slipped in behind me.

I took up a position at the side of the front door, Silas still at my back. The windows on the first floor all had their curtains drawn, but the door itself had a glass insert and a pair of sidelights. A faint light shone from somewhere deeper in the house, just bright enough for me to make out a few details. I was expecting a horror show. I got a showroom.

From what I could make out, the interior of the house was...nice. Homey. The kind of place that should, by rights, smell of cookies and be filled with children's laughter. That somehow made the thought that a cold-blooded killer lived there all the worse. There was a fairly standard lockpad by the door, with a red light indicating that it was, in fact, locked. And probably alarmed. Shit.

"Perhaps I could be of assistance, Detective," Silas whispered. "I have a way with electronics."

I remembered how easily Silas had entered my house, and how he seemed to disappear from surveillance cameras. I nodded and edged to the other side of the door, trying to stay out of the framing of the sidelights. "See what you can do."

I was too far away to tell exactly what Silas did, but he started just like anyone else trying to open the door—he placed his palm on the sensor pad. Ordinarily, if you weren't a registered occupant of the house, that action would have resulted in nothing. Instead, there was a slight beep. It took a moment for the reason behind that to dawn on me. Silas was a synthetic, and legally synthetics weren't people. They were things, and things completely incapable of hurting anyone. But they *were* things that were often tasked with a variety of menial labors, like deliveries and cleaning.

I had never used synthetics—or anyone else for that matter—to take care of my dirty work. I wish I could say it was a matter of purely standing on my principles, but really, it was as much about my own antisocial isolationism as anything. I did my own cleaning, my own laundry, my own cooking because I didn't particularly like to be around other people. I knew it all stemmed from Annabelle, and the past few days had made me realize that it was, at least in part, a way to hide from what I knew about the world. If I was constantly alone, I didn't have to see or think about the injustice around me.

I realized now, however, that there must have been some list, somewhere, of synthetics and agencies that had access to...well, damn near everything was my guess. I was once again staggered by the casual reach that so-called humanity had ceded all too willingly to the synthetics. It clearly wasn't universal access—if it was, the door would have opened for Silas and he wouldn't still be busily typing away, exercising, no doubt, that "way" he had mentioned with electronics. But how many agencies, businesses, and corporations had services that required synthetics to gain access to private dwellings? Cleaning agencies, certainly. Delivery agencies. Personal chefs. Child care. Companionship. Repair services. Even prostitution. The list was endless. Did anyone—even people with some knowledge of the truth, like Fowler—even think twice before blindly signing terms and conditions that likely granted an entire stable of synthetics full access to their homes?

The possible violations of privacy were staggering, and tempered only slightly by the notion that synthetics could do no harm. Except, Silas had done harm. If he had a gun, could he have pulled the trigger as easily as he had thrown the wrench? It would only take a single shot to end a life. But just as I had when I realized the potential information network available to the synthetic population, my worldview underwent another spiraling shift. If they could overcome their programming, even enough to do that single trigger pull—oh hell, or plant a bomb—how much damage could they wreak?

With a soft buzz, the door panel flashed green. I motioned for Silas to stay behind me and pushed the door open. The interior was dark, save for that soft glow coming from somewhere deeper in the house. It was a maze of rooms, the space subdivided in a way that completely ignored the more modern, open style. Whoever had it rebuilt, had done it to the original cramped, multiroom specifications. Maybe it added some kind of charm; for me, it turned the place into a nightmare of blind corners and shadowed hiding places.

I moved through the downstairs as quickly as possible, checking every room and closet, every nook and cranny that looked big enough to stash either a bad guy or a little girl. Zero joy. The light had proven to be coming from the kitchen, a simple fluorescent bulb left on above the range, but no people or any other indication that people had been through recently. The house had three separate staircases leading to the second floor. I picked one at random and began the process anew. Same cluster fuck of rooms stuck together seemingly at random. All the furniture was expensive, and looked pristine. The whole place felt more like a show house than a place where an actual human being lived. Of course, Fowler was a pretty damn far way from human, but still. The vibe didn't exactly scream "serial killer," either.

Different floor. Same results. Nothing.

"Perhaps an attic?" Silas whispered.

We ransacked the upstairs again, looking for any entrance into an attic. We found it, at last, in the ceiling of a closet. Stealth had gone right out the window, and I shoved armfuls of clothing at Silas in order to reach the pull-down ladder. It unfolded and, gun leading, I climbed up. As my head broke the plane of the ceiling—or was it floor?—I panned my flashlight around. Boxes. Dust. Insulation. No missing synthetic. No little girl.

The joists were exposed, thick two-by-eights evenly spaced with no flooring atop them. A couple of inches of foam insulation filled in the gaps between the lumber. The space was huge, running the full length of the house, hot, humid, and all-around unpleasant. But it was also, for the most part, empty. I still pulled myself all the way up, picking my way carefully from beam to beam, checking behind boxes. "Arlene?" I called softly, not expecting—or getting—an answer.

After sweeping the attic, I made my way back downstairs, where an expectant Silas waited.

"Anything?" he asked.

I shook my head, sliding my pistol back into the holster at my waist. "Nothing." I felt an uncomfortable weight settle around my shoulders as I said it—the weight of a little girl's life. "You should have let Fowler take the shot."

"Then you would have been dead, Detective. And the little girl would almost certainly have followed. And my people would continue in servitude and slavery that would make the worst despots of past generations blush. No matter what happens, I made the right choice."

"I'm not your revolutionary leader, Silas," I growled. "I'm not your Washington, or Lincoln, or King. I'm a fucking cop, and I'm tired. Why the fuck did you come to me in the first place?"

Silas didn't answer. Instead, he said, "Hope is not lost, Detective. I do not think we were led here astray. The grounds are large, and there are many places yet where we may find what we seek."

"What is it, exactly, that you seek, Silas? Fowler's next victim, obviously. But why?"

He just smiled that enigmatic smile and headed for the stairs.

Bastard.

Chapter 27

The grounds of the house were extensive, probably close to five acres, which, in New Lyons, was practically an estate. There were, as predicted, several outbuildings—a barn, a trio of sheds, and a Quonset hut, the purpose of which was unclear at first inspection. We started with the sheds. The first held landscaping tools, old-school tools that were all sharp blades and pointed tines. Nothing electric, or even gas powered here—all of it was old-school muscle. All the tools showed signs of wear...and of recent cleaning. Given the proclivities of Mr. Fowler, I didn't want to think what nonstandard uses any of them might have been put to.

The second shed stood empty. It was small, barely four feet on a side and six feet tall, looking more like an ancient outhouse than anything, with a bare wooden floor. Though it wasn't locked, there was a magnetic seal on the outside, so it could have been. "Shit," I muttered, as I swept the walls with the light. The wood of the walls, floor, and ceiling was scratched. Gouged, really. In neat parallel lines. Like fingernails would make. There was no trace of broken nails or blood that I could see, but I had little doubt that a person or people had been kept in here at some point. Fortunately, the gouges had had time to fill in with dust and grime and were far too big to be from a child's hand. Not Arlene, then.

Shed number three was a nauseating repeat of shed number two. Bare and relatively clean, though with evidence of anxious prisoners who had desperately sought escape. Any escape. "Would a synthetic have done this?" I asked, shining the light over more fingernail marks.

"It depends," Silas replied. "If ordered to stay here and be quiet, most would have little choice but to obey."

"He wasn't keeping synthetics, then," I said.

"Not necessarily, Detective," Silas said. Something in his voice made me turn to look at him. His pale features held a measure of disgust that I hadn't yet seen, despite all we had been through. "But there are many subtler ways to cause us pain. If a synthetic was ordered to wait they would have no choice. If they were ordered to do everything in their power to escape, they would also have no choice. I would not put it past a man like Fowler to issue such orders. Even if successful, the poor soul would have no real recourse but to escape and then go report the results to Fowler, likely to be locked up all over again. Perhaps with a better lock."

That thought hadn't occurred to me. I was more acquainted, I supposed, with the straightforward aspects of physical torture. But if a victim had no choice but to obey, to what depths could the depraved mind sink in order to feed their dark passions? Annabelle's existence had been a hellish cocktail of sexual and physical abuse. How much worse could it have been, had her nominal parents been more of Fowler's ilk rather than their run-of-the-mill psychosis? "I'm glad that fucker's dead," I said.

"Me, too, Detective," Silas replied. "But he is one among many. One of the worse ones, I'll grant you, but by no means unique."

"Fantastic." I slammed the door on the shed, closing off the sight, if not the images, of the nightmares contained within.

We continued our search, moving to the Quonset hut. It was a largish structure, probably a thousand square feet with rounded sides, like a soup can that had been cut in half lengthwise. The building was made of steel, and no effort had been taken to give it a more homey appearance. It would have looked at home on a military base or in an industrial yard. Within the confines of Fowler's estate, it looked out of place. It felt wrong.

The door was once again possessed of a modern magnetic lock. Silas immediately placed his hand upon it.

Nothing happened.

"That's unusual," he said.

"What?"

He didn't answer, his attention focused on the touch screen. He was tapping away at it, fingers flicking and swiping. A frown started on his face and pulled down into a scowl. "It's not connected to anything. No network connection at all. It requires a pass code, but there are no overrides. It may as well be a padlock."

Padlocks got a bad rep. Sure, they were old-school technology, but these days, more people could hack a computer than pick a mechanical lock.

"Can you open it?"

"I don't know, Detective. I'm trying."

"Fine. Keep trying. I'll clear the barn."

I headed to the building, which, like everything, seemed neat and well maintained from the outside. No locks on the doors, big sliding affairs that, when I shoved against one, moved with surprising ease. The dim interior revealed six stalls, which, rather than being home to horses, seemed to be used as storage. There were stacks of plastic bins, the lids wrapped round and round with duct tape. Each bin had a valve sticking out of the top, sealed around with caulk and more tape. There were dozens of them, all unprepossessing gray plastic encircled with gray tape. There was something about them that was disturbing, almost ominous. The entire place stank. It was a musty, acrid odor. It reminded me of roadkill, not at the height of stench, but at the point when the decomposition is mostly done and the air has an aftertaste of decay.

I reached into my pocket, drawing forth the knife that I'd taken from one of the attackers back at the docks. I should have been berating myself for forgetting to turn it over into evidence, but instead I flicked open the blade, and moved to one of the bins.

The steel sliced effortlessly through the tape. The lid made a sound like Tupperware as I popped it from the edge of the box. The smell of death hit me like a hammer, ten times—a hundred times—worse than how the barn itself smelled. I staggered back, gagging and coughing, fighting desperately to choke down the bile that was rising in my throat. Panting and gasping, swallowing the rush of saliva, I leaned against the wall of a stall and tried to recover my composure.

It took a good thirty seconds before I regained control.

I drew a deep breath. The smell of rot and decomposition and worse wasn't gone, but it had decreased to the point where it didn't induce the immediate urge to vomit. Day-old roadkill. I approached the bin again and, using the tip of my knife, pried the lid off.

I was expecting to find a body. What I found was more like a soup. Or maybe stew was a better word.

It had been a body, at some point. There were identifiable bones visible here and there, poking up out of the morass of...something. I couldn't identify it, except to call it slime, or maybe ooze. Bodies do strange things when they decompose. Under the right conditions, they liquefy. The purpose of the valve on top of the box was suddenly clear—a release valve for the gasses produced by decomposition. And the source of the smell in the barn.

I backed away and forced my mind to other places, other pastures. I couldn't think about what I was breathing, about those boxes—those *dozens* of boxes—all with their duct tape seals and outgassing valves. I had known

Fowler was insane, but I'd believed him to be a sort of manageable insane. The kind of crazy that was bent to a purpose—in Fowler's case, the purpose of cleaning up Walton Biogenics' mistakes. Hired by the company to take care of any "factory defects" or whatever the fuck the suits called them. But those bodies, those "mistakes" were discarded, left to be found and destroyed by the various cleanup crews. This was something different. This wasn't Fowler's job. It was his personal collection. He wasn't just some corporate hit man. He was a killer, a predator who hunted for sport. Maybe the remains gathered in the bins were all synthetics, which would make him a psychopath, but under the strictest interpretations of the law, not a murderer. But I doubted it. There was no way someone who could do this would be content with those who could never offer even a token resistance.

Either way, this was someone who had needed to be put down.

I wanted to find Arlene safe and sound and—God forbid—not in one of these boxes. But a secret part of me was glad I'd ended Fowler's miserable life. I wasn't proud of it. It actually brought more of the nausea rushing back. But as I surveyed Fowler's macabre sepulcher, I couldn't shake the thought.

I did a quick look into the other stalls. Four were filled with the same boxes. I revised my count of Fowler's victims upward again. There might well have been hundreds of boxes stacked there. They had to be synthetics, at least most of them; if that many "real" people had disappeared it would have popped on the NLPD's radar. How many Fowlers were out there? How many synthetics had been slaughtered for sport or to assuage the dark hunger of their masters?

None of this was helping Silas get the door to the Quonset hut opened. If Arlene, or whomever Silas was after, were in here, they were past helping. The final stall, however, was not filled with boxes, but rather housed a compact Kubota tractor. It was a newer model, powered by a hydrogen cell rather than a gas engine, but it looked to have all the trimmings, including a small bulldozer blade attached to the front.

Time to try a different key.

Chapter 28

Silas was still working on the door.

"Out of the way!"

He looked over his shoulder, and then his eyes widened in surprise and his jaw actually dropped.

When I saw that look, I laughed. Hard. Tears-in-my-eyes, doubled-over-the-steering-wheel, fighting-to-keep-my-seat kind of laughing.

I must have looked like a fucking train wreck. Guy in a suit, dirty, bloody, beaten, with bags under his eyes riding a *bright orange* tractor and laughing like a wild man? The mental self-image made me laugh all the harder.

Silas probably thought I'd cracked. Hell, maybe I had. But when you've got a ton or so of crazy-driven steel coming your way, you move. Silas got out of Dodge.

Right before impact, a horrible thought flashed through my head. What if Arlene was standing on the other side of that door? I took the pedal off the metal, but it was too late.

I was thrown forward against the steering wheel. The fact that I'd been hunched over it with a debilitating case of the giggles probably helped, at least insofar as the steering wheel was driven into my gut rather than having me go careening over it into the door. The sharp force drove the air from my lungs and cut my laughter short.

I sat gasping for breath like a landed fish while staring through tear-blurred eyes at the Quonset hut.

It had a very good door. I couldn't be entirely sure, but I didn't think the tractor had done more than scratch the paint.

Fortunately, that marvelous door had been set into a wooden frame that had, in turn, been bolted to the steel of the Quonset hut. I hadn't hurt any of the steel, beyond maybe bending a bolt here or there, but the force had been enough to tear the entire wooden frame from the rest of the building and send it crashing to the floor, along with the door it housed.

"Have you lost your mind, Detective?" Silas demanded.

I couldn't answer. Still didn't have the breath. I waved a hand at the now open door and fumbled with the pedals until I managed to back the tractor up a few feet. I felt the meaning was clear enough: *mission accomplished, now get your ass in there.* He gave me a long look, but then hurried into the building.

I didn't wait for little things like being able to breathe again. I toppled off the tractor and staggered in behind him.

And then stopped. And stared.

The Quonset hut was all one open room, probably a thousand square feet of usable floor space. It had been tiled—floor, sloping walls, ceiling—in a stark white ceramic that reminded me of a cheap public restroom. There were four stainless steel tables, of a kind I'd seen all too often at the city morgue. Two of the tables were occupied.

One held a girl at that awkward age between childhood and the first blush of adulthood that seemed all elbows and knees and insecurity. It was Hernandez's daughter. She was strapped down to the table, without a stitch of clothing and staring at the door with stark, wide eyes. My first panicked thought was that we were too late, and I was staring at a body, but no, her chest rose and fell and those doe-like eyes were still bright with life. She was alive. And she was absolutely terrified.

But that wasn't what had made me stop.

The second occupied table held a woman. Young, probably in her later teens. Her face was turned away, as if she did not want to see whatever might have come crashing through the door. Her head had been shaved, and I could quite clearly see the skin tag that marked her as a synthetic. She, too, was completely naked.

She was also very noticeably pregnant.

Which was impossible.

"Yes," Silas hissed, with an exultant note of satisfaction.

It occurred to me that we were both standing in a destroyed doorway leering at a pair of naked, helpless girls. OK, not leering. More staring in stunned shock. But from their perspective, it probably looked like leering. And one of those girls was a scared kid. For the moment, I put the entire idea of a pregnant synthetic—*impossible, cannot happen*—out of my head, and rushed to the table where Hernandez's daughter was strapped down. "It's OK, Arlene," I said. "I work with your mom, OK? I'm Detective Campbell." I flashed my badge out of habit, but I was already looking around the room for something to cover the poor girl. The bloodied and befouled rag of my suit coat was clearly not an option.

"My mom?" The words were barely above a whisper, but there was a note of longing and hope that was, quite simply, heartbreaking.

"That's right, Arlene." She was held to the table with canvas straps. They were cinched down tight enough to leave red, irritated-looking indentations in her skin. The only thing she could move was her head.

"Let's get these off of you, OK? Don't be scared now. It's over." I could hear Silas speaking softly with the other woman, too softly to make out the words. I didn't hear any fear or panic, though.

The straps probably had some sort of catch or release, but I wasn't going to make a scared little girl wait while I fumbled about her naked body looking for a release mechanism. Instead, I flicked open my knife.

I hesitated for a moment. Those straps looked tight. Maybe tight enough to restrict circulation. "Are your arms and legs asleep? Numb feeling?"

She nodded.

"OK. This isn't going to feel very good, Arlene. Pins and needles like when your foot falls asleep and you try to walk around on it. You know what I mean?"

She nodded again. "I'm ready. Please. Just get me out."

"Here we go." With a few quick slices I severed the straps.

She gasped and immediately tried to curl into a ball on the table, numbed arms moving in an awkward attempt to shield her nudity. "Just a minute more, Arlene, while I find you something to wear. Then we're getting you out of this hellhole."

"Detective."

I turned to find Silas offering me a white, hospital-style bed sheet. The pregnant synthetic was sitting up on the edge of her table, a similar sheet draped casually around her shoulders, but doing little to hide her nudity as she rubbed at her own arms and legs in an effort to restore blood flow.

"Thanks." I took the sheet and covered Arlene. She clutched it tightly around herself. Then she looked at me with fear and hope and the tiniest bit of shame all warring across her face. "I have to go to the bathroom."

It was such a normal thing to say or want or need that I almost smiled. But I knew that smiling would be the exact wrong thing to do. "Can you walk yet?" I asked instead.

In response, she levered herself up on the table and tentatively eased off the edge. For a moment, she teetered there, and then took one tottering step. She nodded. "Can we maybe hurry? That asshole put us there a long time ago." She hesitated. "You maybe don't need to tell my mom I said 'asshole.'"

I did laugh at that. "Special dispensation, kid. I think she'd be OK with it. And we can hurry just as much as you can. Unless you want me to carry you?"

"No!" she said immediately and with feeling.

I nodded. No doubt she'd had more than enough of strange men picking her up. "But maybe I could lean on your arm?" she added. I smiled and offered it to her.

Silas had the other woman up as well. "Are you OK?" I asked.

"I can walk," she said. Her voice was soft, musical. Pretty. As were her features, with that eerie symmetry that said she had been either a toy or someone slotted for the service industry. I didn't ask about the pregnancy, not yet.

"Let's get you ladies into the house. There are bathrooms, food, and water and, with a touch of luck, we'll find something a little warmer than bed sheets."

"What if the asshole comes back?" Arlene asked.

"He won't be coming back, child," Silas said. "Not ever again."

She tilted her head in thought. "Good." She smiled, and it was like the sun coming up.

* * * *

Fowler's house had three bathrooms. I helped Arlene to one while Silas escorted the young synthetic to a second. Then I made my way to the third.

I needed to clean up. Wash off the blood. Bind my wounds.

I needed to sleep.

Fuck. I needed to call Hernandez. Arlene was probably desperate to see her mother, or at least hear from her, and God knew Hernandez was probably climbing the fucking walls by now, since no ransom request had come in to her.

I couldn't though. Not yet. I knew she had to be freaking out. I knew she'd be pissed when she found out I had waited to call. But as soon as I made that call, half of the law enforcement officers in the parish would descend upon Fowler's lair. And then they'd find the pregnant synthetic. I couldn't let that happen, so Arlene and Hernandez both would have to wait for an hour or two more.

I wasn't sure what would happen then. And I needed to talk to Silas about it. And the girl. And Arlene.

I shook my head and stripped off my jacket and shirt, leaving me in a plain white undershirt. The blood from the slashes on my arms had dried and scabbed, and pulling the scabs away with the cloth sent sharp jolts of pain across the wounds. I welcomed it, since it worked better than caffeine to clear the haze of exhaustion.

There was hydrogen peroxide in the medicine cabinet. No gauze, but a little rummaging revealed a box of butterfly bandages. I took both and set to work. Pulling away the scabs had hurt. Washing the slashes with some hand soap and one of Fowler's towels was unpleasant. The hydrogen peroxide was a special kind of fun. I managed, just, to keep from screaming. The butterfly bandages couldn't quite cover the slashes, but they helped press the wounds closed. I didn't bother to put the shirt or jacket back on—both were ruined anyway, and there was a certain adolescent satisfaction in leaving them lying on Fowler's floor. The evidence techs would want them anyway. There was no hiding the fact that I'd killed Fowler, and no way I could mask where I'd found Arlene, either. Besides, the techs needed to comb through the…remains…in the barn. Try to identify them. Since I doubted Fowler was only murdering synthetics, maybe give closure to some poor families out there.

I stared at myself in the mirror for a long moment, mostly not even seeing the tired reflection that was looking back at me. I was stalling, and I knew it. There were questions that had to be answered and decisions that had to be made.

Time to get back to work.

Chapter 29

We gathered in the living room, though that seemed an odd moniker to apply to anything in Fowler's house. Arlene and the synthetic woman had found a mishmash of clothing, none of which appeared to be large enough to fit Fowler, and sat on a floral-patterned couch. Silas settled his bulk into a recliner—again, though at least this time it wasn't *my* recliner—leaving me to slump into a love seat.

"When do I get to go home?" Arlene asked. "I need to see my mom." She sat with her knees pulled up to her chest in an oversized sweatshirt with three Greek letters stitched across the front. The letters were stitched in a pastel pink. I tried not to think about the fact that its former owner was probably residing in a plastic bin in Fowler's barn. That made the sweatshirt evidence, and I shouldn't have given it to the girl, but fuck it. My career was done, anyway, and even if it wasn't, I didn't think anyone would give me shit about finding some clothes for a scared little girl.

"Soon," I said. "We just have to figure some things out."

"What is to become of me?" the pregnant woman asked. "Silas says I'll be safe. That my child will be safe." She said the word with a certain amount of scorn, as if safety were some sort of fairy tale. Given that she had the unearthly beauty of a toy, it almost certainly had been.

My mind still struggled with the fact that she was pregnant. That wasn't supposed to be possible. It did, I thought with a slight twist of my stomach, explain the state in which my murder victims had been found. The evisceration had been brutal, and no doubt Fowler had enjoyed it, but it also rather effectively removed the physical evidence of pregnancy. Pregnancy. It had to be some sort of anomaly, some sort of freak genetic accident. But how did Walton know? How could they send people like

Fowler to clean up before the world knew? I filed that question away—I doubted anyone here had any answers. "What's your name?" I asked.

She just stared at me. I looked at Silas, who shrugged his heavy shoulders in resignation. "OK. Names aren't important. I'm a cop. I'm supposed to call everything in and get a million response vehicles here in the next ten minutes. They would sweep Arlene off to her mother and then probably to a hospital. I'd be tied up with Internal Affairs and the feds for...hell, until they find a way to suspend or fire my ass. I have no idea what they would do with you, or Silas." I paused. Silas didn't look particularly concerned. The woman looked tired and on the perpetual edge between angry and terrified. "But I'm not going to call them. Yet."

I turned my attention to Silas. "You knew we were going to find her?" I half asked, half stated, waving one hand tiredly at the pregnant synthetic.

"Yes, Detective," he replied. "It was my sincere hope that we arrived in time to find her alive and...unharmed."

"And the other women? The...mutilated ones? They were pregnant as well?" I still couldn't believe the words, even as I said them. Synthetics, male and female, were sterile. It was one of the reasons they were called "mules"—that and being used for manual labor. Everyone knew that. Just like everyone knew they weren't people.

"Not just pregnant. Impregnated by their 'owners' or 'users' or whatever piece of human filth decided to attack them." He said the last with a snarl of anger that made Arlene flinch back.

That snarl took me by surprise as well, enough so that it took a moment for his words to sink in. I think, on some level, I knew that was the case. Of course a young synthetic female was most likely to be impregnated by a human male. Even those not designed and marketed as toys were used by their owners. But the biological implications...

"Proof, Detective," Silas said. "Proof that humans and synthetics are the same species. Oh, not so ironclad that the hard-liners won't trot out examples of horses and donkeys, but proof enough. Proof that we are not things. And if the child proves fertile, which I believe he or she will, provided they live long enough, a proof so incontrovertible that any arguments against it will amount to sheer sophistry. Interspecies breeding is a genealogical dead end, Detective. This young lady"—he gestured at the pregnant woman who still had not spoken—"for all the trauma she has suffered bears the proof that synthetics and humans are one. It is only a tiny spark, but in the darkness that is the lives of most synthetics, a spark can burn as brightly as the sun."

"A spark can also light a fuse, Silas. A fuse that leads to the biggest single powder keg the world has ever known."

"And would that stop you, Jason? Stop you from protecting that child or her mother? Would the fear of what might be stop you from doing what you know is right?"

It was the first time Silas had used my given name. It was such a simple thing to do, to call a person by name, give them an identity beyond what they did, or what their perceived value to society was. It was completely disarming and, at the same time, made Silas seem far more vulnerable than I had ever seen him.

"No," I replied simply.

"I am glad to know I chose the right person for the job."

We lapsed into silence, each of us no doubt contemplating what came next. I looked at Arlene. "Do you understand any of this?" I asked.

She shot me the kind of contemptuous look that only a twelve-year-old girl could master. "Since the lady is pregnant, it means she's a human. Duh. And that means that *all* the synthetics are humans. Which means the rest of us have been acting like—special dispensation—total assholes for a long time."

Without a word, the woman reached over and pulled Arlene into an embrace. There were tears rolling down her face.

"You can call me Evelyn."

The words were barely above a whisper, probably only meant for the girl's ear, but I heard them anyway. I doubted it was her given name, or even the name that she had originally chosen for herself, but then, it seemed appropriate. Evelyn. Eve. Mother of the human race. Or at least, a mother who is of the human race.

I looked at Arlene. "So you understand that, at least for a little while, it's really important that you don't tell anyone about any of this? That you stick to the story of not having any idea why the Fowler person kidnapped you and not mention anything about Evelyn to anyone else?"

She gave me that "oh my God, adults are so dumb" look again and said, distinctly, "Duh."

It was a "duh" that warmed my heart. Whatever she had been through, it looked to me like Hernandez's daughter was going to be just fine. The rest of us, though? "You've been the man with the plan all along, Silas. What now?"

"Now, Detective? Now we change the world."

* * * *

Silas's penchant for dramatic declarations aside, there were any number of details that demanded resolution. The first, and not so insignificant, was getting Silas and Evelyn the hell out of there. An obvious synthetic and an equally obviously pregnant woman could not go walking through a neighborhood like Fowler's in the wee hours of the morning without drawing some sort of notice—the kind of notice that tended to be remembered once a swarm of cops descended on the place.

I'd left my cruiser at the precinct and dismissed the cab. Which put us in an odd spot. We needed a vehicle, but didn't have one. If the NLPD bothered to pull up my travel records, they'd be able to track every ride I'd taken. So far, I could explain all of them. Probably not well enough to keep my badge—gallivanting off to meet, and subsequently shoot to death, kidnappers pretty much guaranteed that ship had sailed, and that was before the whole overthrow-society-as-we-knew-it shtick even came into play—but enough to keep out of jail, at least. If they pulled those records, and the last charges they found on my accounts were for a cab that arrived at Fowler's house and then left without me in it, what would they think? Maybe I could play it as a moment of panic, but then coming to the right decision when the cab arrived and calling everything in. After all, in another glaring blind spot, the cab company would show that no people were transported.

In the end, we decided to risk it. We had no choice, really. Silas and Evelyn had to get out of there, and there was just no other way. Before climbing into the cab, Silas handed me a compact screen. "It's clean, Detective. Prepaid. It has one number in it—to another burner. Call that number when you are ready for the next step. In the meantime, I will see Evelyn to safety and set about doing some other things that must be done."

The circus, as predicted, arrived within minutes of my call. I ignored the captain, the feds, my fellow officers, all of it, until I got to see Hernandez rush to Arlene's side, all tears and hugs at the reunion. They were both whisked away in a sea of black EMS uniforms, headed, most likely, for a waiting ambulance and a ride to the nearest hospital. And then probably to a long line of psychologists and therapists. I almost smiled at that thought. I had a feeling the headshrinkers would meet their match in Arlene. That nut hadn't fallen far from the tree and was hard enough to crack teeth.

When they were gone, though, the hordes descended. I got to hear the full pantheon of disparagement. Terms like "lone wolf" and "hero complex" and even "stupid motherfucker" were thrown around with abandon. The feds added a few of their own, with "obstruction of justice" and "willful negligence." There was even one mention about leaving the scene of a shooting, and the term "manslaughter" came up.

That one at least got shut down pretty goddamned fast when I showed the investigators the barn. It was a bad day for the evidence collection team, not only for having to deal with the atrocity that was the plastic bins, but also for the amount of ejecta that spewed forth from the various officers who just *had to* have a look, because *surely* with all their experience, they couldn't be affected by the horror.

It ended, as I'd expected, with me handing over my badge and gun. Well, and all the rest of my clothing, down to my skivvies. Evidence collection. Clad in a New Lyons Police Department sweat suit—the evidence techs always seemed to have a few sets stashed in their truck for just such an occasion—I climbed into my cruiser (recalled when I called in the rest of the boys and girls in blue) and told it to take me home.

My days as a cop were numbered, and I knew it. Suspension would stretch into paid administrative leave, which would, in its own turn, evolve into early "retirement." Without a pension, of course, since I hadn't put in the time, but probably with enough of a "shut up and go away" settlement to live off for a few years. If I didn't rock the boat, of course.

I grinned at that thought. Ever since I'd planted a knife in the murdering heart of Annabelle's "owner," I'd gone out of my way to keep the boat nice and level. I'd grown complacent, channeling all my anger and bitterness into *protecting* that fucking boat, first as a soldier, then as a cop. Sure, I'd stayed dry, but all around me people were drowning, and I—and every fucking other person along with me—had sat and watched. No. Had enjoyed it. Because, hey, it kept us safe and dry.

I was done playing nice. I was done being complacent. Silas thought he could change the world. He was probably kidding himself. The people—the "real" people—had all the guns and money and training. They had the weight of decades of "tradition" and a quality of life for the average working stiff that approached utopic levels. Provided, of course, you were one of the people that counted as people. All the odds were stacked in their favor, and what did Silas have?

A pregnant woman. And the truth.

It didn't seem like much. Hell, it didn't seem like close to enough. But somehow, it was. Enough for me, anyway. Enough to set a spark. And a spark could light a fire. And a fire could change the world.

It was time to change the world.

It was time to rock the fucking boat.

Epilogue

Detective Melinda Hernandez's House

December 31

23:58

Melinda sat on her couch, glass of red wine in hand and her wall screen tuned to the ball drop in Times Square. One arm was curled around Arlene, snuggled up against her on the couch. Her daughter had long since fallen asleep, but so far she didn't seem to be experiencing any of the nightmares that had plagued her in the weeks since that fucker Fowler had kidnapped her. There wasn't a power in the world that could have made Melinda move and risk waking her.

She took a sip from her glass and stared at the screen, tuning out the insipid commentary from whatever celebrities du jour were hosting. She couldn't keep up with them anymore, a surer sign that she was getting old than the few strands of gray she found in her hair from time to time. She stared more at the giant countdown in the upper-left-hand corner of the screen, and waited. Around the world, people waited, with her.

In minutes, the old year would be gone. The new year would be ushered in. A time of rebirth and regrowth would begin. Every eye was glued to a screen where broadcasts from iconic vistas promised countdowns to a new beginning.

With only minutes to go, those screens flickered and jumped, blurring momentarily into an almost forgotten static. Melinda frowned, but she didn't move, didn't let sound the curse that came to her lips. She didn't want to wake Arlene.

When the picture resolved, there was the image of a man. He was a remarkably normal-looking man. Not pretty enough for video, surely, and with a certain sadness, a certain tiredness, about the eyes. He was, one would think, a man who had *seen* things, who had experienced things that had left their marks upon his body, and perhaps, even deeper. Melinda felt something twist in her stomach, and a strange sense filled her. Was it excitement? Or foreboding? She couldn't be sure, but she recognized Campbell's mug staring out of the screen at her.

For a full five seconds, Campbell remained silent, just staring out from the screens with his dark, soulful eyes. Melinda had no doubt that, in the short-attention-span world, nearly everyone else watching tried to change to a different station, a different site. Out of curiosity, she set down her wineglass and did the same, flicking her fingers to cycle through the stations. Campbell was everywhere.

"What are you doing, *hermano*?" she whispered, still conscious of her sleeping daughter.

Almost as if in response to her words, he began to speak.

"My name," he said, his voice as tired as his eyes, "is Jason Campbell. You don't know me. No reason you should. I've done a lot in my life. I've been a soldier. I've been a cop. I've taken lives and saved them. I've earned commendations and condemnation along the way. But mostly, I'm just a guy, just a human being, like all of you out there listening to this."

He paused, a troubled expression passing like a cloud over his face. "And I do mean all of you. You see, we've all been lied to. It's been a big lie. It's been the worst kind of lie—the kind that we all wanted to be true. So, we just accepted it. We let it go because it made our own lives better. And as a result, we've become what is arguably the worst society in human history."

He paused again, and Melinda knew where he was headed. Arlene had been quiet when the feds and other detectives tried to question her, telling them only about the man who broke into their home and going near catatonic when asked about the rescue. But she hadn't been able to keep any secrets from her mother. Melinda grabbed her wine again and took a quick gulp. She was about to watch Campbell go from a cop forced into retirement by the unforgiving brass to the city's most wanted.

The camera pulled back and panned over. There, in the frame, was a woman so pregnant she looked about to pop.

"This is Evelyn," he continued. "She might just end up with one of the first babies of the new year. Which is remarkable for more than the normal reasons." The pregnant woman brushed back her short hair and the camera zoomed in. The raised pattern of a skin tag was clearly visible against her pale flesh. The camera lingered there while Campbell continued to talk.

"You see, Evelyn is a synthetic. Not human. A thing." He spat the words, not as curses against the woman, but against any who would call her so.

"Except, the father of Evelyn's child is *not* a synthetic. He is, undoubtedly, a raping asshole. But despite that, we still have the gall to call him human and call this woman a thing. But things don't get pregnant, and even if they did, they certainly couldn't breed with a human." He glanced at someone off camera, and a faint murmur of conversation floated through the open microphone. "The search traffic we're seeing shows that you've already started looking. That you've already found the answer that you know to be true. That you've already started to question the lie."

"Shit, Campbell," Melinda whispered. "Are you really doing this?" Of course he was, the fucking idiot. Noble idiot. But still an idiot.

"The only thing that can breed with a human and produce offspring is, of course, another human. Not a thing. Not an object. Not an animal. Synthetics are none of those things. Synthetics are human."

The camera came back to the man, who seemed to be looking somewhere off screen. He nodded slightly. "A packet of information has just been released. You should see the address now. And...it's gone. Another. Again. They don't want you to know the truth. They're trying to stop this feed. They're taking down the sites where we're posting the truth as fast as we can put it out there. They're trying to prop up a society that has been built on a slave labor more heinous than anything known in our history."

The camera went in tight on Campbell's eyes, and Melinda could see the determination, the righteousness in them. She felt an answering stir somewhere in her gut, a call to action like she hadn't felt since she first decided to become a cop.

"They will fail. If even only one of you manages to grab the information, and repost it, it will get out. It contains medical data, video, test results, a thousand, thousand data points that back up everything I'm saying.

"Some of you already know that what I'm saying is true. You've known for a long time. You've been called a synth-sympathizer and stigmatized. Know that you were right. Keep fighting. Others will be swayed by the information, and realize that they've been guilty of horrible things." Melinda felt a flash of guilt as she thought of her nanny and how she had almost pulled the trigger. "Know it. Understand it. Change it. Some won't want to believe. It will be too hard, too painful to come to terms. Do it anyway. Coming to terms with what society has become is the first step to changing it. Some of you will refuse to believe, or just flat out won't care. You'll harp that the stability of society—even one built on the backs of slaves—is paramount. You'll label me a terrorist. You'll call for my head."

Those sad eyes seemed to drink the light, to take on a far more ominous edge. For a brief moment, Melinda did not recognize the man on the screen. It was a Campbell she hadn't seen, and she was reminded that he never really talked about what he did during the wars. "You're welcome to try to take it.

"The way forward is simple. Free all so-called synthetics from their bondage. Immediately pass laws granting them status as full human beings, full citizens of their respective countries with all rights and privileges pertaining. The full details of our demands are included with the documentation provided."

Campbell smiled. Even in his smile, Melinda could see his exhaustion. The past weeks for her had been tough, dealing with not only the departmental fallout from the events leading up to Arlene's kidnapping, but helping her daughter recover emotionally. It looked like they'd been hell for Campbell, too.

"We are not naive or delusional. We understand that this cannot happen overnight. You have one month. But if February rolls around, and the nations of the world continue to insist that their citizens are allowed to be held in slavery, then may your respective gods have mercy on your souls. Because we will not.

"Take this as fair warning. You have thirty days to redress these wrongs. If not, you will face a war such as has never been fought in the history of this world. You have all the weapons. You have all the money. You think you have all the power. But you are wrong.

"It is a new year, a new dawn. The rights of man—of all mankind—will be restored with it, or we *will* burn it all down and start anew.

"To the synthetics listening, I have this message: Survive. You will be the most likely victims of a barbaric backlash against this message, and for that, we are truly sorry. Don't fight back, even if you feel capable of breaking your indoctrination."

The thought that synthetics could fight back—could physically resist—sent a jolt of fear coursing down Melinda's spine. Was that even possible?

"Endure, as you always have. If you can, flee. Run. Escape. We will find you. We will help you.

"To those humans with a conscience—we ask that you shelter any synthetic you can, whether they were once 'yours' or if they find their way to you by some other means. By this act, you can start to atone."

Another glance off camera.

"I've been informed that the authorities are closing in on our position. Remember: they do not want you to know the truth. But know this:

the revolution has begun. You have thirty days to ensure that it is a peaceful one. If not—"

The transition cut off, leaving the afterimage of Campbell's tired, sad eyes burning in Melinda's brain.

"You're going to help Mr. Campbell, right, Mommy?" Arlene asked.

Melinda looked down at her daughter. When had she woken up? How much had she seen?

After the kidnapping, Arlene had told her all about the nice pregnant lady who had talked to her and kept her from being too scared when the bad man had her. How she had comforted her and assured her that they'd both make it home, somehow. Evelyn. Anyone who would take the time to comfort a scared child deserved better than what the synthetics got. And if Campbell hadn't put his life on the line, Melinda would never have gotten her daughter back.

She reached down and tousled her daughter's hair. "Of course I will, *niña,*" she said softly. "Of course I will."

A new year. A new beginning.

A revolution.

Acknowledgements

This book would never have been possible without the help of numerous people who took a rough and dusty idea and helped me clean it up and turn it into something worth writing. There is an army of people at work behind the scenes creating covers and back copy text and fixing all the little mistakes and a thousand other things besides. Many thanks to all of those individuals.

More specifically, I would like to thank Elizabeth May, my editor, and Laurie McLean, my agent for taking a risk on a wannabe author and lending their expertise to make the book stronger with every edit (no matter how painful some of those edits may have been!)

I'd also like to thank my martial arts instructors, Dai-Sifu Emin Boztepe, Sifu John Hicks, Sihing Trevor Jones and Guro Ron Ignacio, along with my many training partners along the way. Anything I got right is because of these folks. Anything I got wrong is a reflection of my own imperfect understanding.

Finally, and most importantly, I'd like to thank my wife, Julie Kagawa. Writing partner, gaming partner, training partner, and partner in all things.

Look for SINdicate, the next book in The New Lyons Sequence by J. T. Nicholas.

As the deadline for governments to acknowledge the rights of synthetics creeps closer, former New Lyons detective Jason Campbell makes ready to deliver on his promise to do whatever it takes to see the synthetics freed.

In the midst of protests and riots, Campbell and his conspirators are preparing to unleash the first wave of attacks against the halls of power when a body turns up on Campbell's doorstep. Attached to it is a simple message: "I found you."

Don't miss SINdicate. Available wherever ebooks are sold.

ABOUT THE AUTHOR

J.T. Nicholas was born in Lexington, Virginia, though within six months he moved (or was moved, rather) to Stuttgart, Germany. Thus began the long journey of the military brat, hopping from state to state and country to country until, at present, he has accumulated nearly thirty relocations. This experience taught him that, regardless of where one found oneself, people were largely the same. When not writing, Nick spends his time practicing a variety of martial arts, playing games (video, tabletop, and otherwise), and reading everything he can get his hands on. Nick currently resides in Louisville, Kentucky, with his wife, a pair of indifferent cats, a neurotic Papillion, and an Australian Shepherd who (rightly) believes he is in charge of the day-to-day affairs. Please visit his website at www.jtnicholas.com